Bical

Bical

Generations Book II

John Reinhard Dizon

Chapter One

The teenager squeezed the sponge slowly, letting the warm water spill down his arm over his chest as he relaxed in the bathtub that morning. He was loving every minute of it, allowing this day to become indelibly impressed in his mind. He gave himself plenty of time to dress for his interview, a grand occasion that would change his life. He was certain that it would change the lives of his family as well. It was a lifetime opportunity that he had no intention of squandering.

His father, Captain Adonis Dizon, had lived in the *barangay*[1] of San Pedro for the past twenty years. He had been stationed there as an officer in the Spanish Army and enjoyed a life of comparative luxury in contrast to his family's Spartan existence in their native Barcelona. Only the military defeat in the Spanish-American War left Adonis with a choice he had second-guessed over the last couple of decades. He chose to remain in Iriga City rather than return to Spain, and his fall from grace as a displaced person left him bitter and frustrated.

His wife Cytherea raised his five sons as best she could as Adonis worked as a carpenter to make ends meet. He was known throughout the village for his artistry, but it quenched his spirit to be working for men instead of commanding them.

---

1. district

He ruled his sons with an iron hand, but it was hard to prevent his soft-hearted wife from indulging her boys when he was out of the house. As a result, they inherited the high spirits that their Dad once displayed, and Teodulfo was the most high-spirited of them all.

The most grievous blow came a year ago when cholera swept through the village, killing the youngest of the Dizon boys. Grigorio, age two, and Ariston, age one, fell victim to the disease. It was news of his brothers' deaths that gave Teodulfo the will and resolve to remain among the living. He heard his mother crying to the visiting physician that she did not want to bury another son in the family plot. Teodulfo began calling from his room, insisting he was not going anywhere.

"You know I don't like being around dead people," he said flatly.

It was the rallying cry that galvanized the household, a story his mother told time and again in the years ahead. Her older boys, Eugenio and Anselmo, had been working in the sugar cane fields and bringing home more than their father on good days. They began skipping school as a result, and the thought of it all made Adonis sick. It made him more angry and taciturn than ever, and Teodulfo would strenuously avoid mentioning his plans for this day as he sat at the breakfast table.

"Well, look who's up bright and early on a Saturday," Eugenio smirked as his mother set an extra plate at the table. "I suppose the kitchen maids'll be making room on the floor for another pair of hands."

"These hands aren't made for scrubbing, much less chopping sugar cane," Teodulfo blew on his nails and buffed them on his lapel.

"If you ever did a hard day's work you'd be in bed for a week," Anselmo grunted.

"Call it what you will, but I call it a smarter way of making money," Teodulfo shrugged.

"Outsmarting is most of what you do, leading those two friends of yours around by the nose," Eugenio shot back. "I can imagine what goes on at that military compound on weekends. They do all the work and you collect all the money."

"I *know* what goes on up there," Anselmo bit into a piece of buttered toast. "This fellow cheats all of the rest of the galley slaves for their hard-earned wages. You have no idea how many hidings I've gotten him out of. Not for his sake, but for our dear mother's."

"I'm thinking about Mom all the time," Teodulfo scooped his egg in between his pieces of toast. "I want Mom to know her youngest son's not going to be breaking his back for the rest of his life. She's going to see that I'm never going to end up on that hill with my little brothers."

"What did you say?"

The response came as a chorus, and he knew he had put his foot in it again. They were very old-fashioned, and he realized how much so every time he came back from the military sector. It was almost as if they were living in another world here in the neighborhood. It was a bleak, humorless existence in which one worked from dusk to dawn with the sole purpose of putting food on the table and getting through another day. Dreams were for those who slept, and those who slept peacefully were those who were buried in the village graveyard. He had come very close to ending up there, and he would fight to his last breath before he came that close again.

"I didn't mean any disrespect. I just meant I want to see the world, like Dad. I'd like to visit Barcelona one day, you know, get to know my relatives."

"Will you listen to this little clown!" Anselmo scoffed, reaching over to tousle his hair.

"Hey, watch the hair," Teodulfo pulled away from him.

"Watch the hair?" Anselmo exclaimed. "After you used half of Mom's cooking grease to build it up like that? Don't get fresh with me, or I'll stick your head in the toilet and wash it all out for you."

"This is pomade, paddy boy," Teodulfo jeered. "Or can't you smell anything but fertilizer anymore?"

"That's enough," Adonis ordered. "You show respect for your older brother. And you quit picking on your little brother."

"Now, come on, Opong, you finish that at the table. You aren't going out and eat in the streets like a *moro*," Cytherea insisted. Teodulfo responded by wadding up his *taco* and cramming the whole thing into his mouth, forcing it down like a python.

"Truly you insult the *moros*, Mother," Eugenio shook his head.

"And to think you would bring such manners to my father's table," Adonis grunted.

"No, sir, I would arrive at my grandfather's house as a prince among royalty," Teodulfo said proudly.

"This boy's words hurt my ears at this time of the morning," Anselmo winced as he covered them.

"A prince is a man of respect," his father, who favored none with his gaze at his table, fleetingly glanced at Teodulfo. "Broken pride leads to humility, and humility breeds respect. You have not learned the most basic lesson yet."

"Perhaps if you took him to the woodshed once in a while he would learn some humility," Eugenio folded his arms as he leaned on the table, gazing at Teodulfo. "I'd be glad to take him out there for you if you're ever too busy, Father."

"Hah! You and what army?"

"That's enough, Opong!" his mother again called him by his pet name, which rankled his brothers no end. Opong was in the archipelagos, and she thought of him as their remote little island. "If you're in such a hurry to join your friends, then just go!" They clucked their tongues and shook their heads as she walked him to the front porch.

"What was my father's father like, Mama?"

"He was a hard man, just like your father," she gazed out at the dusty streets and the thatched roofs of the cottages lining the road. "I barely knew him. Your father was deployed here shortly after we were married. We had no idea we would spend the rest of our lives here. At first it was like a dream. We were given a villa to live in, and our leaders were confident we would crush the American forces. Our government was overrun by traitors and cowards, and before we knew it, the war was over. We decided to stay here and retire, but we never expected them to move us out of our villa. We never thought we'd end up here."

"I'm sorry, mama."

"For what?" she put her hand on her son's shoulder. "God works in mysterious ways. We started our family here, and one day you will leave here and start a new chapter in our family's history. I have had dreams of you leaving, and they have been more regular lately. You listen to your heart, Opong. If you are to leave the Philippines, then leave with confidence and never look back."

"I'd never leave without saying goodbye, Mama."

"Do as you will, my son," she kissed his cheek before going back inside. "Do as you must."

Teodulfo walked briskly up the street where he planned to meet his friends for the hike across town to the military sector. Iriga City had a proud military history and was where his father was stationed before it fell to the 45th Infantry alongside Tagalog rebels in 1900, ending 300 years of Spanish rule. He thought it ironic that he was experiencing his greatest personal victories in the city where his father had suffered his greatest defeats in life.

"Hey, slowpoke. We thought you were going to catch the streetcar."

Teodulfo's closest friends, Isidro and Hercules, were waiting for him up the corner from his home. Isidro was a slender, studious young man, while Hercules was a powerfully-built streetwise kid. They were all the same age, fifteen-year-olds attending high school together. Teodulfo was acknowledged as the ringleader, though he often got second opinions from Isidro. Whenever Teodulfo's schemes got them in over their heads, Hercules was usually able to bail them out on the street.

"Not a chance. A penny saved is a penny earned."

"Don't forget we have to find out what the deal is with the Whitehouses," Isidro reminded him. "If anything goes wrong, we are out of business."

"You'll never be out of business," Teodulfo scoffed. "There'll always be something for you to worry about."

"You need to start finding yourself some more money games and less sneak thieves," Hercules offered Teodulfo a sip of his flask of wine as Teodulfo held up a hand. "I can't keep fencing all that junk you're turning over. The cops're gonna think I'm swiping it."

"There's a big money game coming up," Teodulfo assured him, producing a deck of cards from his pocket. They all wore guayabera shirts, dark trousers and polished shoes, dressed in the height of fashion. Teodulfo kept them entertained with card tricks, continually fascinating him with his sleight of hand. They could never figure them out and he never revealed his secrets.

Teodulfo was known as one of the best card players in San Pedro as well as one of the best card magicians. Only he never crossed the two pastimes and never would. He believed in his ability as a poker player and would rarely if ever bluff his opponents, much less cheat in a game. The temptation was never there because it was anathema to his personal code. He hated liars, cheats and thieves and would never be mistaken for one.

They set out on their way after Teodulfo did a couple of tricks before Hercules finished the dregs of his flask. They began the three-mile hike across town to the military sector, which normally took them less than a half hour when they made good time. It was important for them to set out with time to spare, as much to avoid the hot sun as to arrive at the same time as the other workers. They wanted to avoid getting sweated up in order to stand out from the rank and file reporting for duty.

Teodulfo had worked for the Whitehouse family for six months shortly after the three friends took the trip across town to the military sector last year looking for employment. There was a never-ending stream of Filipinos arriving at Iriga City each week, and the three friends only wondered why they had not taken the trip across town to apply sooner. The monkey-heads could barely read or write, and arrived at the sector dressed in used clothing. Teodulfo and Isidro stood front and center in comparison, and once they were in Hercules was as good as in as well.

Once again Teodulfo was in a daze as they made their way along the dusty streets. Isidro and Hercules engaged in banter, talking about their upcoming fishing trip, or hanging out at the beach, or gossiping about the neighbors or the other kids at school. They were also fantasizing about visiting Manila and picking up some of the latest clothing fashions from Hong Kong. Teodulfo half-listened, his mind wandering as he surveyed the bleak landscape.

Teodulfo stared into a vacant, weed-strewn lot where four little kids were roasting what looked like a dead baby on a spit. He looked harder and saw it was a monkey. He looked up the street and saw a dead horse lying at the curb, bloated to almost twice its size in the jungle heat. A wagon full of half-rotten fruit came flying around the corner, its back wheel ripping the carcass open. A cloud of horseflies rose from the carcass and engulfed the rotten fruit, descending as a swarm of locusts. They crossed the street and Teodulfo saw four giant rats feasting greedily on a dead cat. As they crossed a small bridge that led them to the main thoroughfare to the military sector, Teodulfo saw a man on crutches hobbling in the opposite direction. He wore a hat and sportcoat, only he was naked from the waist down with bloody diarrhea running down both legs.

"Come on, quit daydreaming," Hercules insisted. "We're going to be running late, and you know that fool at the security gate will give us a hard time if we come in behind the crowd."

The threesome double-timed it to the picket fence between the two storage depots leading to the residential sector where the American military community in Iriga City resided. They were close to the downtown market square as well as nearby river ports that made it a prime area for travel and commerce. The rifleman at the gate watched moodily as the Filipinos made their way into the complex, breaking into a smile when he spotted Teodulfo.

"Hey, hotshot," he called over. "See you at the game tonight?"

"Looking forward to it," Teodulfo smiled back.

"Your lucky street comes to an end, buddy," the guard taunted him.

They stopped in front of the administration building where Isidro was employed as a clerk, double-checking the figures of the bookkeepers and accountants to minimize oversights. He made as much as Teodulfo, who was the houseboy of Retired Colonel George Whitehouse. The Colonel lived in a villa at the far end of the grounds, a comfortable distance away from the neat rows of cottages facing the thoroughfare that bordered the office mall.

"Okay, guys, see you at lunch," Teodulfo headed towards the Whitehouse residence. The hired help had their lunch break at 1300, after the regular lunch hour taken by those living on base. "If they have anything available I'll send somebody over."

"Fine," Hercules grunted. He was assigned to the landscaping crew and toiled under the tropical sun eight hours a day. His only hope was that either of his friends sent word of need for manual labor, in which case he would have the luxury of working indoors under an electric fan. They blew hot and humid air, but it was better than no air at all.

Teodulfo let himself in through the wrought iron fence surrounding the two-story frame residence. It was white stucco with Saltillo tiled roof, surrounded by a beautiful rose garden that Teodulfo helped tend when the inside of the house was immaculate. It was a good reason for him to make sure there was always something to do. He tried to hide out in the kitchen as much as possible, where he did double-duty as the cook once the Whitehouses became aware of his culinary skills.

"There you are. I thought I was going to have to cover for you."

"Yeah, that'll be on a cold day."

Teodulfo looked up at Nora Rivera as he changed from his guayabera to a white button-down shirt and black vest in the small anteroom near the rear hall at the back entrance. Nora was a light-skinned Filipina with long brown hair and almond eyes, a proud bosom and long legs that were highlighted by her black maid's dress. She had eyes for Teodulfo but he had a hard and fast rule about mixing business with pleasure. The biggest reason for workers getting fired was over bickering and personal problems.

"Mrs. Whitehouse will be having friends over for lunch today, and they may be playing bridge this afternoon," Nora informed him as she picked her feather duster out of the small box of cleaning supplies on a nearby bench. "Too bad they're not playing poker."

"Are you going to start with those rumors again?" he winced. "If I spent as much time playing cards and winning money as you think, I wouldn't even need a job. I'd just open a pawn shop on the market square and never lift another finger."

"I could imagine. The windows would be filled with pancake griddles and silverware."

"So are those the missing items security's looking out for this week?"

"Those are the items that always go missing. Anything big enough to fit under a shirt tail," she adjusted her garters, causing Teodulfo's pulse to quicken.

"If they quit hiring from the ghetto, they wouldn't have so many petty thieves running around. There's lots of decent people out there working in rice paddies and sugar cane fields. They wouldn't mind being out here on base."

"Who, like the Dizons?" she chided him. "Your father and brothers would starve to death before bowing their heads to these people."

"Maybe not them. There's others, though. There should be better ways to get work here than having to come up to the gate with hat in hand."

"It worked for you and your friends."

"There's always more than one way to skin a cat," he grinned, though it faded as he thought of the dead cat on the way to work. "That's beside the point. People shouldn't have to grovel like second-class citizens in their own country. All we hear about is the Land of Liberty, the Land of Opportunity. If that's so, how come all these Americans are coming over here to live off the fat of the land? My father says they're no different than the Spaniards."

"You keep running your mouth, and you'll be in the paddies digging ditches before you know it," she said tersely as she picked up a rag and a spray bottle. "May I remind you that these people own this property. You don't badmouth the owners. Once they throw you out, it's over. No politics, no appeal, none of your silly backtalk. You'd better learn to save your opinions for outside the gate."

"Yeah, well, I've got an opinion for you. That uniform looks pretty good on you."

She blushed and frowned at him before heading out the door, and he could see her frown melt into a smile.

He had some doubletalk she had not even heard yet.

Chapter Two

The weekends were a special time for the teens as their employers normally allowed them to spend the night at the base so that they could rise early for work on Sunday. They would leave at the end of a long day in order to attend school the next day. Teodulfo, Isidro and Nora all went to school regularly. Hercules, whose family were *moros* with many family members still living in the jungle, attended rarely if ever and spent most of his time on the streets. He made his money selling the wares that other servants lost to Teodulfo in after-hours poker games.

They were like brothers, and anything they made outside of their wages got split three ways. The servants were always purloining items to wager at the games, and Hercules was the only one tough enough to go out on the street and sell them. They pooled their money for Teodulfo to wager, and what he did not win in the first game he would recoup with interest in the return game. When they made extra, they left it Isidro to lend money to people in the office complex which they repaid with interest. Their money was always growing, and Teodulfo and Isidro had the green thumbs to ensure it continued to do so.

Earlier that day after the chores had been done and Mrs. Whitehouse's bridge group had left, the Whitehouses had their dinner before the Colonel retired to his drawing room for his newspaper and cigar. Teodulfo asked for and received an audience with the Colonel, and had spruced himself up to appear quite dapper as he presented himself before Whitehouse.

"Well, young man, what is it you wanted to see me about?" Whitehouse relaxed in his overstuffed armchair, clad in his wine-red robe, his white hair slicked back and his gold-rimmed pince-nez glasses perched on the end of his bulbous nose.

"Sir, I heard rumors about the coming reassignment of military troops here in Igina City," Teodulfo cleared his throat. "There's word that you and your family may be relocating to the United States this winter. Lots of officers have been taking about being home before Christmas."

"That's true, young Dulfo, that's true," Whitehouse thanked him for lighting his cigar. "Rest assured we'll have made arrangements for any contingency well ahead of time. If I receive notice of any relocations, you can be sure that I'll not only find you another position, but provide you with excellent references beforehand."

"Colonel, my friends and I have heard that Colonel Richard Sibley is being transferred to Manila. Since he will have to recruit a whole new staff, we wondered if we might be able to go with him. I could be his houseboy, Isidro could help him with his paperwork, Hercules could do his landscaping and even Nora could work as his maid."

"Hmmph," Whitehouse contemplated the notion. "Well, it is quite possible that many of us may be returning to the States. World politics is changing so rapidly, our commanders don't know where the next challenge will come from. As you know, I've been acting in an advisory capacity here with the Volunteer Forces. They have been talking about sending me to Europe to act in that capacity, and my wife is in love with the idea of living in Paris. Have you and your friends discussed this with your parents? Manila is about six hours from here. If you were to take these positions, you might be required to relocate and transfer to school up there."

"Sir, I can assure you that we are just as anxious to see Manila as your wife looks forward to seeing Paris."

"It sounds as if you and your little friend have put some thought into this. Tell you what, I will make a call to old Sibley and see what is on his mind. If he is relocating to Manila, I will certainly put in a good word for you. You're a good boy, Dulfo, and I'm sure you'll do well."

Teodulfo was walking on air when he met with his friends that evening after supper. They were in their guayaberas and decided to stroll around the river market before Teodulfo headed off for this evening's poker game.

"Yes!" Hercules crowed exultantly. "This is unbelievable luck! Can you imagine what my mother and father will think? Why, we have government advisors coming by our home every other week asking if any of our relatives are taking part in any insurgencies. They think my entire generation is a horde of savages waiting to charge out from the jungle and destroy civilization. Their son in Manila? I can't wait to see the looks on their faces!"

"I'm going to have to break the news to my own parents," Isidro was morose. "My money's been helping the family get by. I suppose I can send money home, but they will miss me around the dinner table."

"They could tie a monkey to a baby chair and not know the difference," Hercules took a sip from a bottle of wine. He offered them a swig but they declined.

"I'm looking forward to seeing the looks on my father and my brothers' faces when I tell them the news," Teodulfo nodded. "I'm just hoping my Mom takes it well. After losing my little brothers, I'm not sure she'll be so happy about me leaving. She's kinda held me tight the last couple of years. I'm thinking I'm gonna have to break the news to her before I tell my Dad and my brothers."

"I thought you mentioned something about your Mom having dreams about you leaving," Isidro mentioned.

"Yeah, maybe it's just me. Maybe I'm hoping she can't let go that easy. It'd be pretty bad if you left home and no one missed you. I know they miss my little brothers."

"Aw, poor little Opong!" Hercules teased.

"All right, deadbeats, ante up," Teodulfo grunted. They fished inside their pockets and came up with $10 apiece.

"Don't spend it all in one place," Hercules scowled. "Or bet it all on one pot."

"Not to worry," Teodulfo slipped the bills into his wallet. "It's a return match from last time. I got these guys down pat. I got a high roller, two by the book buttholes, and a rainy day plunger. The sergeant's the kind of guy who bluffs on a pair or better. The by the book guys clean up his garbage all night. The rainy day guy smells blood once in a while and he'll go all in when he's got a solid hand. They keep me on my toes but unless they dump trash on me all evening, I should have them squeezed dry by midnight."

"You know what you're doing," Isidro was confident. "Do what you do best."

They walked him to the hacienda of Corporal Miller, a black man from Harlem in New York City USA. He had been a gambling man all his life, and when he made the acquaintance of Sgt. Harry Potter, they decided to set up a Saturday night game. Miller had served under General "Nigger Jack" Pershing during the War, and his Bronze Star and Purple Heart gave him the credentials to successfully request transfer to the Philippines where he knew a black man stood a better chance of getting ahead. Hooking up with Potter, a man who only saw the color of green, was a stroke of fortune. They would talk privates into joining the games, and finally they found a couple who became regulars. Getting the house boy to join them increased the challenge.

Potter heard about Dulfo Dizon through the grapevine and knew that he was a formidable opponent who always came to the game with sufficient funds. He also knew that the house boy would cause the others to grow reckless out of pride, which would improve his own chances of cleaning up. He sat in a jeep outside Miller's cottage just outside the military sector where Dulfo was instructed to meet them.

"Hey, kid," Potter called out the window as Teodulfo strolled down the brick walkway to Miller's home. "Change of venue. Hop in, I'll drive you out there."

"Where to?" he asked warily.

"Little Flip joint down the way. They say they'll put up food and drinks for a ten spot. Two bucks a piece, all you can eat and drink, beats the hell outta Miller having to shell out."

"I guess so," Teodulfo climbed in. It was going to be a charitable donation on his part. He was a teetotaler and was too edgy to eat during games.

They drove down about a mile to a barn in a clearing outside the woods. There was a group of Filipinos hanging around outside, and Teodulfo realized that Hercules would have fit in well with this bunch. Potter parked near another jeep and a couple of beat-up jalopies, then led the way inside the barn. It was set up with a counter by the door and a dirt floor leading to a plywood-covered space in the back area. Cold-eyed Filipina women sat at the bar eyeing the newcomers as Potter brought Teodulfo to the table.

"Okay, gentlemen, dealer's choice, quarter ante, same as last time," Potter broke out a fresh deck. "Everybody shell out the two bucks for the refreshment. Draw for high card gets first deal. Let's get it on, boys."

Teodulfo stuck to his game plan. He had read about someone named Lao Tzu who was a great source of inspiration to the ethnic Chinese that comprised a large portion of the Filipino population. He wrote that one should always exploit an enemy's weaknesses and avoid their strengths. Potter was a man who played like a sledgehammer, investing heavily when he perceived an advantage. Almost anytime he showed a pair on top in a stud poker game he would raise one dollar. Teodulfo knew there were fifty-two cards in the deck, and in a five-hand game of seven card stud that would mean that a maximum of fifteen cards would show in each game. If one of the cards he needed were to appear in anyone else's hand, Potter's chances decreased dramatically. Teodulfo pressed hard when he knew one of Potter's cards were unavailable, and it worked well three out of four (seventy-five percent) of the time.

Park and Brown, on the other hand, would not bet against a better hand regardless of the situation. Teodulfo played them accordingly, and if a face card appeared on the table and they remained in the game, chances were they had a pair or better. They did not stick around for many raises, but when they did they were dangerous. Teodulfo and Potter both had a strategy of playing against the kitty, in which they pressured opponents when their pile of chips were beginning to dwindle. When Park or Brown were on the losing end, they could be persuaded to fold if the odds of willing were unfavorable. However, if they stayed the course, it was fairly certain they could back their wager. It was sufficient reason to cut one's losses.

Corporal Miller was extremely cautious though he threw it to the wind when he had one too many drinks at the end of the night. His pile of chips tended to grow at first, then would shrink back to normal once his fortune levelled out. He and Potter appeared as a couple of rams when that happened, the Sergeant seemingly affronted by Miller's brazenness. He noticed that Miller would make the fatal error of focusing on beating Miller and did not pay mind to other potential threats on the table. Teodulfo was as a sparrow swooping in and swiping morsels from bickering doves, which netted him a couple of large pots.

The midnight hour soon approached, and Teodulfo cashed in seventy-five bucks which was a nice score for the evening. That would be twenty-five dollars for each of his friends, a nice return for a ten-dollar investment. He was in high spirits when the game broke up, and they all shook hands as they returned to their vehicles in calling it a night.

"You did well tonight, boy," Potter said grudgingly as they made their way along the bumpy road back to the military sector. "Been playing long?"

"A couple of years, sir. I watched people playing on the street and learned, then began teaching my friends. I started saving my pennies to play with the adults, and soon I was playing well enough to get invited back."

"Do you rely on skill or luck, in your opinion?"

"A bit of both, sir. If I had to do without one or the other, I'd rather not play."

The guard at the fence waved them in, and Potter came to a halt in the shadows of one of the storage warehouses.

"Well, I wish you a good night, sir," Teodulfo said as Potter switched off the engine.

"One moment," Potter turned to him. "A word before you go."

Nora heard a scraping at the door of her cabana at about 0300. She was concerned that it might have been a wild animal, and crept slowly towards the screen door with a baton in hand. She peeked through the shadows and perceived someone sitting on the steps.

"Teodulfo!" she was alarmed as she recognized his pompadour through the screen. "Is that you?"

"I didn't mean to wake you," he replied wearily. "I just need to sit here a minute."

She knew something was amiss and she rushed out in her nightgown to his side. She gasped as she saw the swelling on the left side of his face and knew he had been assaulted.

"Omigosh," she reached over and touched his chin with her fingertips. "What happened?"

"Some guy gave me a ride to the poker game, then robbed me when we got back. Let me get up and clear my head."

Potter asked him if he had cheated during the game, and Teodulfo was offended in strenuously denying it. He then mentioned that he expected some gratitude for driving him to the game and wanted a couple of bucks for gas. Teodulfo said he would settle up at the next game, and Potter called him a dirty Spaniard.

"I know your father," Potter hissed venomously. "He was a coward and a deserter. He decided to stay here after the war and live like a king. He never thought he'd die here like a dog."

"My father was a captain. You'll never amount to more than a sergeant."

Potter doubled him up with a sinking hook to the stomach. He desperately sucked wind, trying to stay on his feet as Potter rifled through his pockets. He found Teodulfo's roll and stick it in his pocket.

"Don't let me see you at the game again," Potter warned him. "If I put out the word you've been cheating, you won't find a game on a military installation anywhere."

"Go to hell," he spat, resulting in the punch to the side of the head that dropped him to the ground. It resulted in the bruise that Nora was tenderly treating with a bowl of soapy water an hour later.

"You mean he stole all your money?" Nora was upset. "There must be something you can do. Why don't you speak to the Colonel, maybe he can approach the fellow and get at least some of it back."

"I've got bigger things going on," Teodulfo revealed, and told her of his plans to get jobs for the four of them in Manila.

"You never said a word to me about this," she was taken aback. "We've hardly even spoken, much less planned for the future. How can you just expect me to leave my family and go to Manila?"

"I was hoping we could work out the details as we went along," he winced as she applied ointment to his bruise.

"Details? You don't even know me. You've never asked me out on a date or anything. All you do is hang out with your friends and play cards on weekends."

"You're the best part of the day here," he admitted, gazing into her eyes. "No matter what the weather's like, or what kind of day I'm having, I always know that if I look at you it changes everything somehow."

"Why didn't you ever say anything? How come you never talk to me?"

"You're always busy, and I'm always busy. Besides, I wanted it to be the right time. I didn't want to seem like one of those guys who go around flirting with every girl they meet. I wanted to wait for a time when we could be alone and talk to each other. I didn't expect to have to get beat up for the right time to happen."

"So when do you think all this is going to happen? How am I going to break the news to my mother and father, and my brothers and sisters? My whole family's here in Igina City. If I move to Manila, I'll only be able to see them a couple of times a month. I'm not sure I'm ready for this."

"You'll be able to do far more for your family in Manila than you can here. This is the *barrio* here, Nora, we're just a step away from Jungleland. Manila is the nation's capitol, we can make connections there. You might be able to find jobs for your brothers and sisters up there. You might even be able to move your parents up there, who knows? Even if they don't go, surely they want more for their daughter than this. You're young, you're beautiful, you're smart, you've got a wonderful personality, they've got to have higher hopes for you than this."

"My gosh, Teodulfo, where is all this coming from?" she blushed. "Thank you for saying you think I'm beautiful."

"All you have to do is look in the mirror, you don't need me to tell you. Besides, I'm sure you hear it a dozen times a day."

"There's a difference. I don't hear it from you."

"That's why you've got to come with us," he brushed her satiny locks away from her lovely face. "With you at my side, I can do anything. It's going to be a big challenge for all of us, but once we get situated we can start making new plans. Don't you see, Nora, this is just our first step. We've got our whole future ahead of us. Isidro and Hercules and I, we've been together since we were little kids. We stayed together for a reason. And when I first laid eyes on you, I knew you were special. I knew you were going to be one of us somehow."

"I don't want to be just another one of your friends, Teodulfo."

"You'll never be just another anyone," he reached up and cradled her face in his hands. He sat up on the cot he was reclining on, pulling her down into his arms. She sank to her knees alongside him and suddenly he pulled her face towards his, snaking his tongue between her lips. She gasped in surprise as he slipped off the couch and knelt alongside her, taking her into his arms. His blood simmered as he could feel her body beneath her nightgown, clad only in her panties. He took hold of her breasts as she moaned in passion.

He remained with her until sunrise, the loss of his winnings and the beating by Potter the furthest thing from his mind.

Chapter Three

Teodulfo had major problems that Sunday after slipping through the Whitehouses' back door before sunrise. He got a couple of hours' sleep before rising to prepare breakfast for the Colonel and his wife. After they left for church, a dreamy-eyed Nora assured him she would get lunch started while he caught another quick nap. Just as she said, she had a sumptuous meal on the stove by the time he woke up and took over in the kitchen. The middle-aged couple were in a jovial mood when they returned and complimented Teodulfo after their meal. He bade one and all farewell before he took off to meet his friends to deliver the bad news.

"That filthy dog!" Hercules raged when he explained what happened. "Point this fellow out to me and I'll beat him to an inch of his life!"

"Sure you will," Teodulfo snapped. "And ruin all our plans to go to Manila. Don't you think they would hunt you like an animal afterward? We'll get it all back and more when we make our move. We need to cut our losses and wait for our next opportunity."

"He's right, Hercules," Isidro agreed. "Violence isn't going to solve anything. We have to use our heads now. If Whitehouse is going to put in a good word with Colonel Sibley, we would be foolish to make a rash move."

"Twenty-five dollars would have put food on my family's table," Hercules hissed.

"The money would have done a lot of good for a lot of people," Isidro insisted. "Everybody's having a rough time right now. The Americans are trying to make things better but it takes time. Things are going to get better in Manila before anywhere else, and that's where we need to be if we want to help our families. We can do more damage by retaliating against that Potter fellow. We should cut our losses and focus on our long-term goal."

"Where are you getting these big words and big ideas, the comic books?" Hercules sneered. "I'll crack that fellow like an egg and get our money back, and we'll have some spending money up there in Manila."

"Isidro's right," Teodulfo was adamant. "I'm right. You need to cool down, let me make this move. Our lives will be changed when we get to Manila, I guarantee it."

"And what will happen when our lives begin to change?" Hercules demanded. "You'll be the house boy and Isidro will be the office boy. I'll be out on the streets doing dirty work. The day will come when you won't want anything to do with someone doing dirty work, and it'll be a long way back from Manila for me."

"That's the stupidest thing I've ever heard," Teodulfo grew angry. "We've been together since grade school, and you've stood up for us back when the big kids were trying to steal our lunch. When we got old enough to figure things out, every time we got hold of a good thing we always shared equally. It's always been all for one and one for all, just like in the story books. You two are like brothers to me. You've been closer to me than my real brothers. It's almost insulting to hear you talk like that. How could you be arguing about settling a score for someone you're expecting to stab you in the back?"

"Well, since you put it like that," Hercules said grumpily.

"How could you even think like that?" Isidro was upset. "There has never been a time when we ever thought of you as less than a brother! Your words have cut me to the heart."

"All right, all right!" Hercules growled. "Now that we've got that out of the way, I'll hold my peace and let Teodulfo continue his scheming. If we can make more money in Manila, then let's go for it. I'll let Harry Potter keep his ill-gotten gains, and only wish he knew how lucky he is that I'm not coming to even the score!"

Teodulfo's next obstacle came in breaking the news to his family. His father was cynical as always but secretly hoped his son would get the break he needed. His brothers were derisive, largely due to envy in wishing it was they who had gotten a chance at Manila. Only his mother was somewhat encouraging, yet she was grieved at the thought that she might be losing her youngest living son well before his eighteenth birthday.

"Mom, everything will work out fine," he assured her. "I'll be able to send you something extra every week, more than I'm giving you now. Plus, with money I'll be able to take time off and come to visit on weekends. I'll be able to take you downtown for lunch, and buy you pretty clothing."

"And what is that supposed to mean? My cooking is not good enough for you anymore? I suppose you don't care for the way my clothes look on me either."

Mrs. Cytheria Dizon was arguably the most beautiful woman in the San Pedro district, so much so that it took her a long time to make friends when they first moved into the *barrio*. She had waist-length coal-black hair that was streaked with gray, and emerald eyes that offset ivory skin stained by the jungle sun. It was her Christian spirit and giving heart that eventually endeared her to her neighbors and kept the flames of romance burning in Adonis' soul.

"Surely you're kidding," he scoffed. "I'm known as the best cook on the base, and my food tastes like scraps from your table in comparison. Plus, you would be the loveliest woman in Iriga City even if you were dressed in a horse blanket."

"Flattery will get you nowhere," she stifled a smile. "So are you going to abandon your schooling? Are you planning to remain a house boy all your life?"

"Of course not, Mom. There are lots of schools in Manila, a lot more than there are here. I can easily attend classes during the daytime while the Sibleys are at work. You know how Isidro is, he studies every chance he gets. He'll be pushing me every step of the way, and I'll be thinking of you all the time I'm in school. I know you want me to get an education even more than making money. I'm not going to be selfish, I'll want to make you proud."

"You have my blessings, my son," she cupped his chin in her hand, gazing into his eyes. "Make me proud."

And so it was that Teodulfo and his three friends arrived in Manila that Saturday evening. Nora had the toughest time of all convincing her parents that the move was right for her. Nora's parents invited the Dizons to their home for dinner that week to confirm that they had actually bought into Teodulfo's scheme. His parents were very surprised to hear that Nora had become romantically interested in Teodulfo. He never mentioned anything to them, seemingly interested only in his friends and his cards. Señor Rivera was very magnanimous throughout the evening and continually toasted both families as well as the success of their son and daughter.

Teodulfo's brothers were astonished that he had attracted the attention of such a lovely girl as Nora, but were content to know that they might end up with such a sister-in-law. Teodulfo, in turn, was greatly distressed by the fact that everyone was anticipating such an event. His pique was exacerbated by his discussion with Nora as they sat out in the garden behind the Riveras' house after dinner.

"You made me bleed the other night," she said softly.

"Are you kidding?" he was alarmed.

"Do you mean to say you thought I had been with other boys?" she was indignant.

"Why, no," he objected. "I just didn't think of such a thing, that's all. I hope I didn't hurt you or anything."

"Well, it won't go back to the way it was, if that's what you mean. A girl hopes that their first one will be their last."

"It looks like your parents are good with this move," he quickly changed the subject. "The Colonel assured me that the Sibleys are expecting all of us, even Hercules. If we work as a team, we'll be able to hit the ground running. You and I will turn on the charm and get the house in ship shape, and Isidro will make himself indispensable as usual. Hercules will get out on the street and make connections, and before you know it Manila will be our oyster on the shell."

"I'm sure you realize how nervous I am," she laid her head on his shoulder as she sat alongside him. He grew uncomfortable, but the scent of her freshly-washed hair and her perfume was highly stimulating. It was all too hard to resist, and soon he had his arm draped around her shoulder.

"There's nothing to worry about," he kissed her head. "Hercules is watching our back, and believe me, there is no one worse to have against you. His family are Moros, you know. Half of them still live in the jungle. They are completely uncontrollable. In fact, I think I'm the only one he even listens to."

"I don't care about him," she held his hand. "I want you to be watching over me."

"You know I will," he replied. He looked down at her doe-like eyes and her ruby lips, intoxicating in the moonlight. He was drawn like a bee to honey as his mouth pressed down against hers. Only he glanced up towards the house and noticed silhouette in the window, and suddenly he felt very, very uneasy.

Things would be a lot more comfortable when they were in Manila at last.

It was an hour before the ship was prepared to set sail for Manila, and Teodulfo was nervously awaiting Hercules' arrival as the passengers began lining up at the loading dock. He had messed up before on occasion, but this would be unforgivable. Teodulfo could probably come up with an elaborate excuse as to how Hercules got sick, but there would be a major problem if he showed up at the Sibleys' home with a contradicting story. Further, there would be no way to contact Hercules at his parents' hooch. If they left without him, Teodulfo would be under enormous stress in cleaning up this mess.

While Teodulfo nervously paced the dock along the outskirts of San Pedro, Harry Potter was stumbling towards the door of his cottage along the outer perimeter of the military residential sector. He had been deep in his cups this evening when he heard the crisp knock, and hoped it wasn't someone on official business. Although he was off-duty, he didn't need anyone going back to base wisecracking that Sgt. Potter was drunk again.

He threw open the door and saw the neatly-dressed Filipino in his guayabera shirt, khaki slacks and highly-polished shoes. His shaggy hair was slicked back, draping his powerful shoulders, and in his hand was a neatly-wrapped box.

"*No tenemos trabajo aqui*," Potter growled. "You're at the wrong house, buddy."

"I was sent here by Teodulfo Dizon. He asked me to bring you this package."

"What, are you nuts? Take a hike, monkeyhead."

"He's leaving to Manila this evening. He asked me to explain that this is an old Filipino custom. When someone leaves his hometown, he always sends a gift to someone he may have offended so that the spirits bless his voyage. There is money and a token inside. If you take the money but return the token, then he is blessed and his trespass is forgiven by the spirits. If you take the money and the token, then he will know that you have also forgiven him. I will come back in the morning to retrieve the box. If you keep the box as well, then he will know you have blessed him and wish to remain his friend."

"No, you stay the hell away from here," Potter shot back. "He can think whatever he wants. I'll keep my cigars in this box, and whenever I smoke one I'll think of that slopehead getting lit up."

"Have a good evening, sir," the massive young man departed.

He did not go very far, reaching the end of the block before stopping short beneath the shadow of a nearby eucalyptus tree. He watched as the front light in the cottage went on, and he tiptoed back across the tiny lawn where he positioned himself at the corner of the house. He waited until he heard the loud scream he anticipated, and scurried back across the lawn in heading back towards the main thoroughfare en route to the downtown wharf.

He was quite sure that the black krait snake inside the gift box did the job intended.

* * *

It was about midnight by the time the foursome arrived at the Sibleys' villa. It took the cargo ship about six hours to circle the coast in arriving at Manila, and one of Sibley's servants was waiting for them in an Army jeep. The youngsters were somewhat queasy after the long ride, and it was well past their normal bedtime. Yet they were both nervous and excited as the Colonel met them outside the villa in front of the cabanas behind the house.

"It's great to have you young folks here, welcome to my home," Sibley grinned broadly. Richard Sibley was a tall, broadshouldered man with a gray crewcut and piercing blue eyes, having the stately bearing of a man of authority. "I'm glad you had a safe trip. I can have sandwiches brought out to you if you'd like to have a snack. Of course, we'll be having breakfast in a few hours, and you'll get a tour of the house and be briefed on your duties at that time."

"No, we'll wait, thank you, sir," Teodulfo knew what the expected response was, to Hercules' consternation.

"You could've at least ask for a damned banana," Hercules growled as they headed for the cabanas. There were three structures covered by mosquito netting, and Nora took the one on the right while Teodulfo and Isidro opted for the middle cabana. Hercules had one to himself as his pals knew he tended to snore and pass gas while asleep.

"And set myself up for monkeyhead jokes? No way. Get some sleep, we'll chow down tomorrow."

The youngsters were summoned to the villa at 0600 where they met the matronly Mrs. Sibley, who regarded them with the condescension of royalty. They were next escorted to the kitchen area where they were given uniforms by one of the servants. Teodulfo and Isidro were given stewards' jackets while Nora got a skimpy maid's costume, Hercules receiving a linen shirt and overalls. Isidro would be on loan to the Administration Center on base during the day, while Teodulfo would be in charge of the kitchen as well as the two servants who tended to the villa. Nora would be in charge of keeping the house tidy, and Hercules would attend to landscaping along the property lines. It was much along the lines of their assignments in San Pedro, though they earning twice as much at five dollars a week.

They were very excited about being in Manila, and took walks towards the city square at the end of each day. The talk of the town was the Pensionado Act of 1903, which allowed Filipinos to emigrate to California USA and participate in government-sponsored educational programs. The purpose was to return the graduate students to Manila as community leaders across the nation, but it was well known that most would leave the program and head out to find their own place as migrant workers in America.

Things seemed to be going well for them, but at the end of the second week Teodulfo suspected something was amiss when he was called into the Colonel's study. He knew that the officers considered that their inner sanctum where even their wives knocked before entering. He straightened his black bowtie and smoothed his shirt, dusting his black jacket before knocking on the thick oak door.

"You wanted to see me, sir?" Teodulfo cleared his throat as he stood at attention alongside the Colonel's plush armchair.

"I regret to inform you that there's been a change in plans, boy," Sibley stared at the far wall. "We ended up on a very short list for applicants to be reassigned to the States before the end of the year. I'm afraid the Whitehouses won't be the only ones going home for Christmas."

"But—why, sir? I thought the government was making some big changes over here."

"Too little too late. It's too damn hot here, for one thing. Plus there's too many shortages, the roads are terrible and the political situation is far too unstable. But I did make an offer, and I intend to honor it. I'm willing to bring the three of you with us, but not the girl."

"Why—why not?"

"It's about the missus, to be frank. She has a jealous streak."

"When—when do we set sail?"

"We're looking at Friday night. It's a take it or leave it proposition for everyone."

"I—I'll have to talk it over with the others, sir."

"Not good enough, boy. I know you speak for the rest of them, so the choice is yours. They want an inventory list and the number of passengers I'm submitting by 0800. There's twenty other officers on line behind me who would board ship in an hour's notice."

"All right," Teodulfo's voice quavered. "We're in."

"All in," Sibley grinned in using the poker term. He was well aware of Teodulfo's reputation as a gambler, which why he was sure the young man would take his chances. "I'll reserve steer-age space for three on our voyage scheduled for Friday at 0600."

Teodulfo was as a zombie in shuffling back to the cabana that evening. Nora and the others had had a long day in the 110-degree heat and were already preparing for bed after filling up on drinking water and showering.

"So what's the deal?" Hercules sat on his cot in his cabana as Isidro was propped in the rickety chair alongside him. "Are we digging an irrigation ditch tomorrow?"

"I wish," Teodulfo said shakily, then told the two boys of his discussion with Sibley.

"Holy cow," Isidro was stunned. "We won't have enough time to tell our families."

"It's now or never, guys. We can be in America by next week. The choice is yours."

"We've come this far," Isidro stared at the floor. "We can't back down now."

"We'll become rich men in America," Hercules was elated. "It's the chance of a lifetime. To hell with Manila, America here we come!"

Teodulfo gave them a limp handshake before returning to his cabana. Betraying Nora was the least of his concerns.

He knew deep down he would never see his mother again.

Chapter Four

"Isn't this grand! Isn't this truly grand!"

"Looks a lot like the Binondo District in Manila. You see one, you've seen them all."

It was nearly two weeks later by the time Teodulfo and his friends arrived in San Antonio, Texas in the United States of America. It took them nearly a week to sail from the Philippines to Hawaii, then to California from where they took the railroad to their final destination. They helped the Sibleys unload their truckloads of furniture and carry it inside the two-story villa just off North New Braunfels Avenue after three days on the train. It was a long and arduous journey, but once the weekend came and they got their day off, seeing was believing.

They did a lot of walking that first Sunday and got a general idea of what the demographics were about. North New Braunfels was mostly retired military and their extended families. South New Braunfels was lower class whites, Mexicans and blacks, as was most of the property west of Fort Sam Houston. The military base was the nexus of the community that defined the north central area of the city. Broadway was the main thoroughfare along the west end populated by people of all races, colors and creeds. They walked down Broadway after wandering around downtown and visiting the Alamo. It was here on Broadway where they knew they would get their start.

Hercules had not been overly impressed by the downtown area, or at least no more than he would let on. It was the Broadway area that impacted them all, particularly due to the significant number of Chinese restaurants and laundries along the boulevard. The Chinese had constituted forty percent of the population in the Philippines, and it stood to reason that if they could make connections here, then so could they. The boys would infiltrate their network, see how it worked, and go from there.

Teodulfo also knew that the Chinese were hardcore gamblers, as were enlisted men with time and money to burn when they were off-duty. Between interacting with the soldiers on base and stopping here and there for cups of coffee at Chinese restaurants, word of a game would surface eventually. At that point, they would officially be in business. Hercules decided to spend his free time here on Broadway to see what he could find, and Isidro would hobnob with other civilian workers on base. Teodulfo planned on working the downtown area where he could take in the sights and mix business with pleasure. Broadway was a short distance away, and he could meet up with the others before dark each evening.

One thing that caused him a great deal of consternation was his Fort Sam Houston ID card. Richard Sibley was the kind of man who called all his house boys George. Teodulfo and his friends were at the medical center getting checkups when his card was being processed, and Richard scribbled 'George' on the envelope in which he sent the paperwork. The adjutant at the Administration Center was swamped with requests from all the new arrivals, and put 'Dizon' as his place of birth and 'Bicol' as his name. His friends laughed themselves silly when they all learned how George Bicol came into existence.

He was not in the best of moods as he wandered along South Alamo Street that Friday afternoon, still feeling sulky over his new name. He was also haunted by thought of his mother and wondered how he was going to resolve that issue. He could send a long letter, but phoning her would be an impossible task. No one would have a phone in the *barrio*, so she would have to be at some municipal building to even have access to a phone. Plus he knew what a horrible experience it was to make calls from the Philippines to America in the best situations. He wasn't big on writing letters, but this was something that needed to get done. He would wait for feedback from his mother before even trying to extend an olive branch to Nora.

He had been touring the Chinese restaurants, standing around out front and stepping inside here and there pretending he was looking for someone. The Chinese were a stoic, taciturn people, weather-beaten by adverse conditions throughout their travels. They were very much the epitome of what was considered Oriental inscrutability, though Filipinos were the exception to the rule. They were loud and boisterous, one reason why the Americans derided them as 'monkeys'. They were also very proud, as more than one overbearing American soon found out.

At length he came across the Cantonese Lounge, an Oriental-themed restaurant replete with a yellow-tiled roof, red walls, stained glass windows and a pillared entrance. It stood out among the seedier places along the street, and since he was hungry he decided to stop in for an egg roll to tide him over until he returned to the base. They had a few customers, most likely tourists or people coming home from work without dinner awaiting them at home.

He ordered it to go at the counter, and as he waited he noticed a well-dressed gentleman seated at a booth by the door. He wore a slicked-back pompadour and a white suit with a dark tie with the top button loosed. He hung his jacket on the pole at his booth, indicating it was his custom to dress well despite the sweltering subtropical heat akin to that of the Philippines. He was reading a Spanish newspaper, indicating he was probably bilingual.

"You from here?" Teodulfo asked him in Tagalog, the native language of the Islands.

"*Si, lo soy*," he answered in Spanish.

"I just got here last week. I'm Teodulfo."

"My name's Apolonio. Have a seat. Care for some tea?"

"Don't mind if I do."

It didn't take Teodulfo long to realize that this fellow was an old school Filipino. He had that elegance about him that the old folks had, the dignity that the youngsters tried to affect on Sundays and holidays. A lot of it had to do with dressing well, but even more of it was about respecting yourself as a person. Apolonio was the kind of fellow that could introduce Teodulfo to the kind of people he wanted to meet.

"Been here long?"

"About fifteen minutes," Apolonio replied, then chuckled at Teodulfo's consternation. "Actually it's been about ten years now. Came here by way of Los Angeles. I was one of the only ones here, but more and more and coming east because of the political situation. It's like they invite you over, then they decide they want you to go back."

"Well, I'm not going anywhere. I sure would like to find out where everyone else is hanging out. I'm here with two of my friend from Iriga City. We got jobs in Manila, but as soon as we got there we got a take-it-or-leave-it offer to come here."

"Aren't you a little young to have pulled that off?"

"Yeah, but that's how it happened. Take it or leave it."

"What'd your parents have to say about that?"

"They didn't. I'd rather not talk about it."

"I see. Yes, it would be a good thing for you to get connected. Look, why not come by here tomorrow evening around six. Not your friends, just you. I'll bring you over to a place where you can meet some people."

"I sure would appreciate that."

When he returned to the Sibleys' villa that evening, everyone else's success was just as marvelous. He found that Hercules' roamings had taken him to the other side of East Houston Street where he made connections with a few Mexican locals at the *cantinas*. Isidro wound up on Broadway near Brackinridge Park where he made the acquaintance of some of the Chinese people who owned businesses there.

"As a matter of fact, I don't know if I'll be staying here much longer," Isidro announced. "The Chinese indicated they may have need of a good bookkeeper. They're not all that familiar with tax laws and the like. They've got so many new businesses started, they want to have someone from their own part of the world to make sure they're not being cheated."

"Yeah, well, I may also have something of my own going soon," Hercules spoke up, not to be outdone. "Those Mexicans like the idea of having someone around who can handle themselves. I'm thinking they may make an offer that can make me some money for watching people's backs."

"Well, that sure is something," Teodulfo mused. "It didn't take long for everybody to make plans to go their separate ways."

"Hey, slow down there, friend," Hercules growled. "Nobody said anything about splitting up. It was your idea for us to go out and make new connections. I said the Mexicans were making offers, I didn't say I trusted them. They only respect me because they know I can't be messed with. I have no way of knowing whether I can trust them to watch my back. That's what friends are for. There's a couple of those fellows I couldn't trust as far as I could throw them."

"I don't like the way you're looking at it either," Isidro agreed. "Those Chinese are very clannish, just like the people back home. I may seem Asian to them, and closer to them than the round-eyes, but that doesn't make me Chinese by a long shot. It's going to be quite a while before I can understand what they're saying behind my back, and I don't want to be left out in the cold if I don't like what I'm hearing."

"All right then, let's clear the air over this," Teodulfo insisted. "That'll be our code, then. It's all for one and one for all, like the Three Musketeers. That's what we'll call ourselves, *los Tres Amigos*, the Three Friends. No matter who we connect with, it'll always be us against them. We'll never let friends, or money, or women, or anything come between us. Let's swear to it."

"Agreed," they joined their right hands. "We swear. All for one and one for all."

And so it was that Teodulfo went forth to meet Apolonio the next evening, reassured that he was not in another take-it-or-leave–it situation. He was dressed well in a new guayabera and crisply pressed pants, shoes buffed to look like mirrors. Apolonio was waiting out in front of the restaurant, and they walked almost ten blocks to East Carson Street to a place called the Corregidor Club. Teodulfo was immediately impressed, not only by the club but Apolonio's inscrutability. He had no doubt that the man knew what an impact this would make on him.

They stepped inside the place with the red and black veneer, Teodulfo finding himself in a place that was enhanced by its Oriental décor. Bamboo and straw was used as trim along the framework, while pictures of the Old Country and families and friends adorned the walls. He was greatly impressed by the fact that the clientele was entirely Filipino, and a pretty barmaid came over to take their order.

They both ordered sodas and sat at a table close to the corner where they could see people coming in and out from across the room.

"This is like a community center for our people," Apolonio explained. "They can come here and speak to others in their own language, reminisce about the Old Country, and maybe even get news from home. People who live in California are in closer contact with their relatives across the Pacific. When they move further east, they find themselves drifting out of the network. That's what causes the overcrowding in Asian communities and creates resentment among their neighbors. All they see is the crowd, they don't realize it's still a small minority."

"It stands to reason that if we improved our communication, we could get word out to people so they wouldn't be stuck on the West Coast. They could come out here and still keep in touch with their relatives. After that, it would be about giving people a reason to come out here."

"I've always wondered about the military base," Apolonio mused. "If we had a connection there who could help us send and receive telegrams, it would be much easier on the people. The Chinese must have a way to communicate, otherwise there wouldn't be so many of them."

"Don't forget, they've been here much longer than we have. I read in school that they were the ones who built the railroads. It stands to reason they have a network that stretched clear across the land. I'm sure we could build one just like it if we had a good plan."

"People say that is the problem with our people, they talk too much. The difference between our people and the Chinese is that we do all the talking and they do all the listening."

"I disagree," Teodulfo sipped his soda. There was one fan in a window and it did not do much to improve the humidity in the room. The subtropical heat was an excellent reason not to carry any body fat that wasn't absolutely necessary.

"If you don't communicate you never get ahead. I know my father was an important man back in Spain. When he moved to the Philippines he had to learn a new language, and he stopped communicating. As his fortunes changed, it got worse. My brothers tried to be just like him, and they were never much for making connections. I saw how my mother was treated by our neighbors, and it was because she was outgoing. I started trying to be like her, and my whole life changed. I made friends with all the kids in the neighborhood, the kids in school, and even all the grownups. Eventually I met the two fellows I came here with, and it was like I had two sets of brothers, two families. No sit, communication is the road to success. I'm only fifteen years old, but I know that for sure."

"It's refreshing to see someone who has conviction in their beliefs. These days it seems like people don't really believe in anything. Maybe it as something to do with the war. For the Filipinos, they got freed from the Spanish, but it's more like they just got new owners. For the Americans, they just got over a Civil War, and then they get this Spanish War, and now there may be another one on the way. The Chinese just try to find different ways to stay alive, just like the blacks. People are just looking for some peace and quiet, and when they cain't never find it, they just stop believing it exists."

"Peace and quiet is for old people," Teodulfo insisted. "You think old people who sit on their porches in their rocking chairs are happy? They sit there wishing they could go out and do something, just one more time. That's how people get old, when they sit around with nothing to look forward to. That's what made my father old. No sir, they can pass the peace and quiet to someone else. I want to be where the action is."

"Well, Mr. Action, here come some of my friends. These are people you can communicate with."

Three Filipino men wearing slicked-back pompadours and freshly-pressed white shirts walked into the lounge and immediately came over to where Apolonio and Teodulfo rose to meet them. Teodulfo was introduced to Santiago from Mindanao, a man of his own height and build with the same pragmatic way about him. Francisco of Quezon was squat and brawny, a man of action much like Hercules. Guillermo from Luzon was a tall, lanky man who was quiet and retiring like Isidro. It was almost as if Teodulfo found their counterparts in San Antonio. Apolonio, who had not inquired, was as amused as the others that Teodulfo was known at Fort Sam as George Bical.

"Why not?" he shrugged as they teased him good-naturedly. "My friend Hercules goes by the name of Luzon. That's where he was brought by missionaries after his Moro tribe was wiped out by the Spaniards. Moro is Spanish for Moor, you know. They said the blood of Mohammed was poisoning the Filipino race. They pushed the Moros as deep into the jungle as they could, and when the Moros fought back they tried to kill them off. Hercules ran away from the orphanage and lived on the streets. He told people he was the mighty Hercules from Luzon, and that became his name. When he'd get in trouble with the police, they could never find the Luzon family so they would just turn him loose."

"Now, let's just hope you stay out of trouble," Apolonio said pointedly. "We try to play it low-key around here, like the Chinese. We have our gambling once in a while, but that's as far as it gets."

"Gambling!" Teodulfo's eyes lit up. "Do they have games here in the lounge?"

"Well, well," Francisco chuckled. "I suspect our little friend was taught to play cards by the soldiers in Igina City. Take care, Teodulfo. There are quite a few sharks in these waters who live for the smell of new blood."

"I'm a barracuda myself," he replied proudly to a chorus of guffaws. "I'd like a chance to see if I can keep from getting eaten by sharks."

"Tell you what," Santiago confided. "Our friend Arsenio is having a game at his home tomorrow night. If you show up here about six tomorrow night, we'll bring you with us. I'll have you know the pot limit is five dollars, so you may be betting your week's wages if you're not careful."

"Don't worry about me, I'm a careful player," he reassured them. "I'm a house boy for one of the Colonels, I work pretty hard for my money. You can be sure I won't throw a week's wages into the wind just like that."

"What about those friends of yours?" Francisco wondered. "Aren't they going to get lonesome with you gone two nights in a row?"

"I'm sure we'll be getting together Sunday. And I'll tell them all about you fellows, I know they'll want to come out and meet you fellows. You see, you'll be getting all three of us for the price of one."

"We'll see about that price at the game tomorrow," Apolonio chided him.

"I'm just grateful that you brought me here to meet your friends. I'm finally starting to feel at home here in San Antonio."

It was the beginning of one of the biggest chapters in his life.

Chapter Five

Hercules had taken to frequenting the Mexican bars at the south gate of Fort Sam Houston past East Carson Street along North New Braunfels Avenue. The military derided the *cantinas* in the area as 'blood buckets' and were declared off-limits to the Fort personnel. Still, the new recruits often snuck in their civilian clothes for a quick drink and ended up going back on payday for an unforgettable time. The Mexicans took care to watch out for the boys, and it was rare that the MPs were called to break up brawls or reel in an out-of-control soldier.

On this particular evening, Hercules Luzon was hanging out at the Depot at the foot of the wooden bridge crossing the railroad track leading to Burleson Street on the other side. He was checking out the action and noticed that a small Mexican fellow was being heckled into playing a game of pool for a beer wager. The Mexican declined but the other three men persisted until he finally obliged. He won a well-played game, but his opponent claimed he did not call his pocket and his friends stood by him. The man grew angry and attempted to leave but the threesome boxed him in.

"I saw the whole thing," Hercules strutted over. "If you don't want to buy the man a beer then you should let him go."

The resulting fight was short. Hercules decked the biggest man with a hard right, causing the other two to scurry away.

"Hey, brother, my name is Celestino," the Mexican introduced himself. "You come on over to La Tuna over on Probandt near South Alamo tomorrow night, and we'll treat you right."

"Sure, I'll bring one of my buddies."

"Bring 'em along. You're a good man, my friend'll be glad to meet you."

And so it was that Hercules brought Teodulfo with him to La Tuna the next evening. It was a spacious lounge with a large patio area where mariachis played for tips and beer. As was the custom, everyone was well-dressed as they came out to socialize this Saturday night. Hercules bought beer and they found a table where they joked around until Celestino made his way through the crowd.

"Ah, my friend, how good to see you," Celestino hugged Hercules as he rose to greet him. He was introduced to Teodulfo, who was going by the name of George Bical on the street. "You two come on over and fix yourself a plate. You have something to eat, then I'll bring you over to meet my friends. There won't be much eating after that."

"You go on over," Teodulfo nodded to Hercules. "I couldn't eat a bite, I had supper before I left the Colonel's house."

"You're skinny as a rail, a stiff wind's gonna blow you away."

"It'd take a typhoon to move you, big lug."

Teodulfo noticed a young lady sitting by herself at a side table and decided to saunter over. She wore a summer dress that accentuated her shapely yet petite figure, and her black hair spilled over her shoulders and framed her proud bosom. Her almond eyes looked inquiringly at the debonair young man as he approached.

"Have you had anything to eat yet?" Teodulfo nodded at the tables joined together where two women were ladling out rice, beans and *carne guisada*[1] onto plates with homemade tortillas.

---

1. beef and gravy

"No, I ate before I got here."

"Yeah, me too," he said, then held out a hand. "George Bical."

"I'm Stella Munoz. Nice to meet you."

"Would you like another drink?"

"No, I'm not a drinker."

"Me neither. Can I sit down for a minute? I'm waiting on my buddy."

"Sure, why not."

She seemed bashful as she averted her eyes, and he appreciated her flawless tawny skin and her ruby lips.

"So, are you from Mexico?"

"No," her eyes flashed. "Are you from China?"

There was a short pause.

"Okay, let's start over. You from around here?"

"Yes."

"Well, I'm from Fort Sam Houston. I work for one of the Colonels there. Actually, I just came over from the Philippines. I've been here for about a month."

"I could tell by your accent."

"Is it that obvious?"

"Well, you've got an accent, and it's not Mexican. And I was only teasing. I know it's not Chinese."

"Lots of different people from lots of different places come through here, I guess."

"Looks like your friend's looking for you."

"Yes, and he's got his new friend right beside him."

"Stella," Celestino grinned. "Looks like you're keeping our friend George company."

"We've got a lot in common. We don't eat, drink or smoke."

"Maybe you can talk everyone else out of it. Come on, come sit with us at the table."

They had put a few tables together in the far corner and covered them with a paper tablecloth. There were several people seated at and near the table, but the seats of honor appeared to belong to a couple of cold-eyed, hard men at its center.

"John, Dave, this is George Bical. He is a good friend of Hercules," Celestino made the introduction as everyone eyed him sternly.

"Thanks for having us," Teodulfo spoke out uncertainly, puzzled at the reception.

"Well, make yourself at home, amigo," John spoke out. "Any friend of my sister's just might be a friend of mine."

George's head spun around as he looked at Stella with fresh eyes.

"They're just giving you a hard time, pay no mind," she insisted.

"Hey, Romeo, go easy on that one," Hercules nudged him as he sidled up to him at the noisy table. "I think I've got a good deal going here. These fellows move stuff from Mexico around the neighborhood. They told me if I could watch some of their fellows' backs, it could turn into some good money. I also mentioned you and your card games, and they said they can get you situated for a slice off the top."

"Is that right? What do I get?"

"They get one opening ante off every pot, and split the take with you fifty-fifty. You run the game, they provide security. They also provide drinks and food, a dollar a man paid at the door. You don't get any of that."

"No sweat. Who do I talk to?"

"Celestino handles business for the brothers, that's John and Dave Munoz."

"Who do I talk to about taking Stella out?"

"Dammit, Dulfo. You better not mess this up. I'd talk to Dave. No, make that John. Well, damn, take your pick."

"I want to take her over to the Corregidor Club. Why don't you bring Celestino along so they think you two'll be our chaperones?"

"Say there," Stella nudged him from where she sat to his right. "Did you think of asking me first?"

"Why, won't you want to go out with me?"

"You're pretty sure of yourself, aren't you?"

"If I wasn't, I wouldn't dare get out of bed tomorrow morning."

It was not long before things were arranged for a date between Teodulfo and Stella. He split his attention between Stella and the table, turning on the charm while watching how the brothers operated. He liked their style, the way everything flowed through them. Intermediates sat on either side of them, and whoever needed something spoke to one of the men. They relayed it to the brothers, who responded with a nod or a shake of the head. Instructions were also passed through the middle man. Teodulfo recognized this as a military-style chain of command. The Munoz Brothers had been doing this for a while, and they did it well.

"So you've got everything figured out, eh?" Stella gazed into his eyes as they took the floor to dance a romantic Mexican ballad. "My brothers are going to let Celestino bring me to that club of yours next weekend. Believe it or not, it's the first time they've let me go out without one of my sisters. Good thing you have it set up for the afternoon."

"Well, that's yet to be arranged, but it'll be taken care of by then," Teodulfo led her expertly around the floor, having been taught ballroom dancing by his mother as a boy.

"My, my," she chuckled. "You just figure everything out as you go along, don't you?"

"I manage to get by. There's one thing for certain I've figured out."

"What's that?"

"I'm not going to let anything get in between me and you."

She leaned her head against his chest as they drew a smattering of applause from the onlookers for their elegance. Teodulfo realized he was going to get along just fine here in San Antonio as the band played on.

* * *

"Okay, I think we're making some real progress here," Isidro said as he brought coffee to Teodulfo and Hercules in his tiny apartment off Broadway near Hildebrand Avenue. He had secured his position with Mr. Wong, a leader of the Chinese community who owned a restaurant, a laundry and a tea room. He greatly impressed Wong with his bookkeeping skills and even had great suggestions that improved the businesses. The tips and tricks he learned while watching the military personnel in the commissaries in San Pedro were paying in spades.

"So let me get this straight," Hercules stared at him warily. "We give you ten percent of what we make, and you invest it in the Chinaman's money loaning business. He charges ten percent, so we get that much interest on our end."

"Exactly," he was enthusiastic as he sat on an armchair facing his friends seated on his couch. "The new immigrants can't go to banks to take out loans, so they go to Mr. Wong. I convinced him that the more he lends, the more he can make. So if you fellows start making good money with your card games, this can't help but blossom. I'm sure of it."

"Here's something you can run by your friend," Teodulfo suggested. "Why not have him let us set up a game for him? We all know the Chinese are degenerate gamblers, they would place bets on a cockroach race. I've got a game going Wednesday night with Hercules and the Mexicans, and Friday with the Filipinos. If you can get us a Monday night game, that'll be profit coming in three nights a week. I'm pretty sure your friend Wong will be able to lend pretty good sums of money out in a short time."

"And what happens if some welcher decides not to pay?" Hercules growled. "Is Wong going to guarantee our investment?"

"I hadn't thought that far ahead," Isidro mused. "It must be similar to our communities back home. I'm quite sure that if someone betrayed such a trust, he would be ostracized by the community."

"That's not enough," Hercules insisted. "Now, back home I know those who lent money usually had friends who would go out and make sure someone made good on a debt."

"I'm not sure what Mr. Wong would think about that."

"Well, let's try this," Teodulfo offered. "If some Chinaman refused to pay, maybe Hercules and one of the Munoz fellows could pay them a visit. They would be able to charge an extra ten percent for the inconvenience. That puts money back in everyone's pocket."

"Now, if the fellow was unable to pay in the first place, what sense does that make?" Isidro scoffed.

"We'll carry a piece of his furniture down to the pawn shop," Hercules sniggered. "And we'll keep going back until the fool is sleeping on the floor."

"It makes a lot of sense to me," Teodulfo admitted. "I don't want to have anything to do with that sort of thing, but at least it'll make for safe investments."

"I think the Munozes are going to be very glad that we came along," Hercules grinned.

Teodulfo only hoped that it would continue to be the case as regarded his intentions towards Stella Munoz.

He was very persuasive into getting Apolonio to front his request in having an afternoon soiree at the Corregidor Club that next Saturday. He won the day by offering to cook the meal at the card game the night before. The Filipinos were delighted with his shrimp fried rice, the like of which many had not tasted since they left the Islands. There was not a man who would have denied his request afterwards, and so it was that the patio was opened for a garden party the next afternoon.

Stella was resplendent in a white flowered dress and sandals, escorted by Celestino who wore a guayabera shirt and black slacks as did most of the other attendees. They were introduced by Teodulfo to Apolonio, who in turn brought them around to meet everyone else. The club generally opened the patio once a month, so they accommodated Dulfo by moving the event up the calendar to this day. As Saturday was generally a day for running errands and taking leisure, word of mouth spread around the community so that most everyone would stop by at one time another throughout the day.

Teodulfo was dressed in a new cream-colored suit that drew compliments from one and all. Isidro was the newest member, and all the girls pointed and giggled at the dapper little man as he joined Hercules at his boisterous table. He looked over slyly and winked now and again, causing them all to break out into a fresh wave of nervous laughter. Apolonio came by once in a while and pointedly asked them if everything was okay.

"We've got to get out of here," Teodulfo muttered as he brought himself and Stella bottles of soda at their table in the far corner.

"We just got here," she sipped her soda through a straw. "Where'd you want to go?"

"We can go up to Austin," he replied. "It's a few hours' ride from here. I know someone who will take us. We can get married the first thing Monday morning."

"What?" she stared at him. "Are you crazy? I hardly know you."

"Listen, I know how these things work. Your brothers are going to keep you under their thumbs until the best deal comes along. By the time I get set up, they'll have already given you to someone else. I've got things going with these Filipinos, the Mexicans and the Chinese. Plus I've got a stable job. In a few months we'll be able to buy a house and start a family. It'll be great, Stella. We need to do this now while we have the chance.

If for some reason they decide against us we'll never have this chance again."

"Hey, back up for a second. You never even told me you loved me."

"Of course I love you," he was exasperated. "Why do you think I want to marry you?"

"Where the heck do you come from?" she squinted at him. "You didn't even ask me if I love you."

"Well, don't you?" he was hesitant. For once he had not thought that far ahead.

"Oh my gosh," she held her fingers to her temples. "This man invites me out for a party, and now all of a sudden I am planning the rest of my life."

"Look, we can make this work," he insisted. "Come with me."

"Geez," she looked around the room, noticing that Celestino and the others were partying hearty and probably would not notice them slipping out. "What am I going to wear?"

"I'll buy you clothes, don't worry. I've got money."

"How old are you anyway?"

"How old are you?" he challenged her.

"Fifteen."

"Me too. We'll be fine."

"Well, I don't know. This seems kinda crazy."

"This will work. When we get back I'll tell Hercules, and he'll back us up. What can your brothers do, kill me? If they don't, we'll buy a house and settle down."

"Well, I'm the youngest. I've got three sisters, and they're all married. They keep talking about getting me out of the house. I don't think it'll be the worst thing in the world to them. They'll just be sore because you didn't even ask their permission. Why don't you go talk to them first?"

"Stella, I'm not Mexican and I'm only a house boy. They'll put us off, I tell you. They don't know who I am and what I'm about."

"You're crazy, that's what you're about. Well, fine, then. Let's go."

Teodulfo signaled to Hercules, and he joined them as they stepped outside onto East Carson Street.

"Look, you need to cover for us," Teodulfo told him. "We're taking off."

"No way," Hercules scoffed. "Her brothers'll kill me. Where you going?"

"We're going to get married. I need you to watch my back on this."

"What?" he put his finger in his ear and shook it. "They asked me to keep an eye on her."

"Look, we'll come back and have a big wedding. You and Isidro'll be the ushers."

"Yeah, if they don't slit my throat and toss me in a ditch. Are you good with this?"

"I'm going with him, aren't I?"

"Unbelievable. How are you getting there?"

"See that fruit wagon there? He's been waiting since we got here."

"All right, then."

Hercules exchanged hugs and kisses with both of them.

"You coming back?"

"I go back to work Tuesday. I'll meet you here Monday at noon and you can bring us to face up to her brothers."

"Yeah, great. I'll surely be looking forward to it," Hercules was sarcastic.

He watched the couple walk towards the fruit wagon, his heart rejoicing that his friend had chosen such a lovely girl for a wife. He resolved that, as always, he would stand behind Teodulfo come hell or high water.

Chapter Six

When Teodulfo and Stella returned from Austin, he got them a room at the Hotel St. George on Crockett Street in the downtown area before calling Isidro at the Szechuan Empire Restaurant on Broadway. It was about two hours later when the desk clerk called to tell him that Hercules and Celestino were in the downstairs lobby waiting for him. Stella and Teodulfo came down to meet them, and they could tell that Celestino was not as sincere with his congratulations. They hailed a coach and were soon on their way to La Tuna to meet with her brothers.

"That was a stupid move you made, Filipino. A damned stupid move," Dave snarled at him as the eight people sat at a table in a far corner of the patio.

"My name's Teodulfo, in case you forgot."

"Teodulfo? You told us it was George," Pete snapped.

"Well, you're my brothers-in-law now, so you may as well get used to my real name."

"We've come up with about a half dozen names for you," one of the Munozes' friends interjected.

"Hey, that's my husband," Stella spoke up.

"You be quiet!" Dave warned his sister, then glanced at his friend. "*Y tu tambien!*"

"All right, the damage has been done already," Pete exhaled. "We've come here to see what we can take away from this and move on."

"What damage are you talking about?" Teodulfo inquired.

"There is a right way and a wrong way of doing things, and what you did is not the right way," Dave flushed.

"*Un momentito, hermano*," Pete raised a hand. "So where are you going to live? You have to come out of that hotel sometime."

"I have a house we'll be moving into on Friday," he was hesitant.

"You *have* a house or you are *looking* at a house?"

"I have a house I'll be purchasing on Friday."

"And that is for sure. You're moving my sister into her own home on Friday."

"That's what I just said."

"Well, okay," Dave raised his eyebrows, looking at his three companions.

"Where is the house?" Pete demanded.

"Off Burleson."

"Where is the house?"

"116 Can't Stop, it's a little frame house with a nice back yard."

"Okay. There has to be a wedding here in town for our family."

"No problem, I'll take care of it."

"When?"

"Give me two weeks."

"We'll set it up. There's a Catholic Church, San Patricio, off the highway. We'll have it there."

"Fine."

They all stood to leave, and the brothers had choice words for her in Spanish.

"Your sisters are going to want to have a word with you."

"Okay, they can come by the house Saturday. We'll have a housewarming."

"I should warm your behind," Dave shook his finger before they all parted ways.

Teodulfo returned to work the next morning, and Isidro found the couple a room on Broadway where they stayed until he got everything set up. Teodulfo was treated very well by the Sibleys, who handed him a $20 for a wedding present and gave him Friday off. He bought a bike from the commissary on base, and was able to ride back and forth from work to the apartment. He also picked up a couple of dresses for Stella, who seemed to be greatly enjoying married life.

"I'm just so worried about us getting together with my family," she said as he prepared dinner on the hot plate in their apartment that evening. "I want everything to be perfect."

"Don't you worry about it," George assured her as he chopped up a tomato and an onion to cook with the bass fish he had been given by the Sibleys. "The Filipinos have put out the word, they're collecting bric-a-brac you can use for decorations. I've ordered a bed and a kitchen table, that's all we need for now. I'm not too bad with a hammer and nails, either. I can put up some shelves until we can buy some cabinets. We'll be fine, you'll see."

"You know, I can handle myself pretty well in the kitchen. I'm not sure I'm going to want you in there all the time."

"I'm sure you can see I do this for a living. In the Philippines, the best cooks are men. I'm afraid you'll have to get used to it."

"Uh-uh, are you looking to get into your first fight?"

"Well, I don't do too well against Hercules," he wiped his hands on his apron, "but I can take you!"

He rushed across the tiny room and tackled her onto the bed where she squealed as he covered her face with kisses.

"My, you're pretty romantic, no one would ever guess," she gazed into his eyes as he rested on her tummy. "Wait until I tell all of your friends."

"You try that and you won't get into that kitchen until you're old and gray."

"Good. So if I don't tell, then you'll stay out of my kitchen."

"I guess we'll see about that."

Teodulfo bought the house as George Bical to protect his privacy, and they arrived that morning at the frame one-bedroom house where the seller gave them the keys. They waited until the truck arrived with the bed and dining room set from the commissary, and the couple struggled carrying their new furniture into the house. There was an icebox and a small cabinet in the kitchen which would help them store food. The seller was kind enough to have left a block of ice in the box, and George decided to go pick up groceries while Stella got acquainted with their new home.

When he returned, he spotted a truck leaving from in front of their house on the dusty street. He cruised up on his bike and saw a number of items out in the back yard. He set the bike up against the post of the overhang at the back door and asked Stella what was going on.

"This is stuff your friends from the Corregidor Club sent over. It looks like you've got more here than bric-a-brac."

Teodulfo marveled as he helped Stella bring in a couple of nightstands, some lamps, a few area rugs and a coffee table. All of a sudden it appeared that all they were missing was a living room set.

"Golly," he chuckled as he gazed around the small kitchen that adjoined the living room. "It didn't take us long to get set up, did it? Say, what do you think you're doing?"

"Mmm, this chicken is fresh," she opened the small packet on the sink counter.

"Get out and stay out," he playfully swatted her butt as he began sorting through the groceries, handing her a soda. "Lunch in a half hour."

"Enjoy your time, Mr. Bical," she wagged her finger. "Things will change."

Teodulfo rose before dawn that Saturday morning and crossed the wooden bridge from Burleson Street to New Braunfels Avenue en route to Fort Sam Houston. Colonel Sibley was in a good mood, telling stories about his own recollections of his days as a newlywed. He headed out to meet his friends for golf, and Mrs. Sibley began preparing for her bridge party after lunch. He set up a scrumptious buffet for them and served drinks at the patio bar until they finally adjourned around 4 PM. She let him go after he did the dishes, and he sped back down the road to rejoin Stella at home.

He was taken aback to see a group of people milling around in the backyard. When he walked the bike up to the overhead, he saw over a dozen Mexicans longing around on lawn chairs, munching on food that was spread over a rickety luncheon table. They spotted him and swarmed over to meet him. He got to meet his three sisters-in-law, Sara, Beatrice and Carlota, who was also known as Charlotte. Their husbands were with them, as well as two other female cousins and their spouses.

"We're leaving the lawn furniture," Charlotte told him. She was the shortest of the three, barely reaching her husband's elbow. He was the only Anglo of the lot, standing 6'2" and weighing a solid 210 pounds. "I got a feeling you'll be needing it."

"Ed Welk," he shook Teodulfo's hand with an iron grip. "My friends call me Butch. We live right up the way on Hays Street. Feel free to stop by any time you like. The girls are pretty close, so I'm sure I'll be seeing you sooner than later."

"Sounds great."

"Have a beer? I set a case on ice in that basin."

"Sorry, I'm not much of a drinker."

"Well, in that case I hope you brought your appetite. That wife of yours set out quite a spread."

Teodulfo went over to the table to see what she had done. Obviously there were more than a few dishes that had been brought along. There were three piles of tortillas, along with *carne guisada*, chicken *mole*, rice and beans, guacamole, and numerous other Mexican delicacies. He smelled the scent of fried food coming from the kitchen, and knew that he had married a worthy competitor.

"Well, Mrs. Bical, it sure looks like you've backed yourself up here," he shook his head as the screen door slapped shut behind him.

"I told you, mister," she came over and kissed him. Her hair was tied up in a bun and she was wearing his apron over a summer dress. If it were not for her family outside, he would have dragged her into the bedroom. "It's our kitchen now."

"Looks like it'll be a question of who gets there first."

"It won't be hard to figure out. You'll have dinner waiting when you get home from work. Sundays I get to sleep in."

"Sounds reasonable to me," he agreed.

Married life sounded like it was going to be pretty comfortable.

* * *

Life in general was picking up for him as the weeks progressed. Stella went to the doctor and confirmed that she was pregnant with a child due in August. Teodulfo was coming out with an average of five to ten dollars a night at the poker games which was always complemented by his winnings. He convinced Hercules to match his donations to Isidro, and it resulted in a $100 bill for each of them around Christmastime. The Chinese money lending operation was bearing fruit, and more people were looking to borrow cash for the holidays.

Teodulfo became very much a part of the Munoz family circle as their favorite cook, and the Bical home the favorite place to visit. He planted a pecan tree out back which he expected to provide a comfortable shade in years to come. He got close to the three sisters and their husbands, and it was not long before they were all announcing pregnancies and getting their own families going. Things had even gotten back to normal with Dave and Pete, and their brother John who had recently gotten out of prison. The brothers started bringing their girlfriends around, and family get-togethers were becoming ever larger affairs. As it turned out, Beatrice and Gilberto Perez bought the house next door. The Sundays at the Bical-Perez lots turned out to be the largest of the monthly get-togethers.

Hercules and Isidro would come by for the Bical soirees, and they would bring their Mexican girlfriends to mingle with the others. Teodulfo would set up lawn chairs near the pecan tree in the far corner of the backyard, and the relatives would privately joke that it was Filipinos-only back there.

"I've got to hand it to you," Hercules sat back, sipping a beer. "You've really made something for yourself here. All this family and friends, who would've thought just a year ago."

"I couldn't have done it without you fellows," Teodulfo reassured them. "I wouldn't even be married if you hadn't watched my back that day."

"You rascal, you would've figured out a way somehow," Hercules playfully gave him a painful shot on the shoulder. I've never met anyone as slick as you. Except our little mathematician here, of course. He makes every month seem like the holidays."

"We can do more," Isidro assured him, calmly sipping his iced tea. "The Chinese network is growing. The Anglos are finding out about it, and they're getting their Chinese friends to borrow for them. The Chinese are charging double for Anglos, twenty percent on the dollar, and they're paying it."

"Yeah, and suppose they don't pay. What'll they do, send a bunch of coolies out to beat up an Anglo?"

"The most an Anglo can borrow is fifty dollars. If he reneges on his Chinaman, the Chinaman gets cut from the network. He can't broker any more loans until the outstanding debt is repaid. All the Anglos who borrow from that particular Chinaman will end up pressuring the welcher so that their connection is restored."

"Sounds pretty foolproof to me," Teodulfo nodded.

"If you guys can get another game going somewhere, we can put more money on the street," Isidro insisted. "Do you think we can get a Thursday night game with the Mexicans?"

"Hey, I'm a married man," Teodulfo protested. "I need to spend some time at home. We just got a radio last week, and Stella likes sitting around with me at night listening to broadcasts. She's already got a problem with the three nights a week."

"You've got a baby on the way. Are you sure you can't use the money?"

"Listen to this cold-blooded tax collector," Teodulfo shook a finger at Isidro. "Wait until you get married, we'll see how that attitude changes."

"Don't hold your breath," Isidro grunted. "I enjoy making money too much."

"You know we have that meeting on Saturday at the Corregidor Club," Hercules reminded them. "That high-roller from Manila's coming in from the Islands. They're having a big welcoming party for him. Maybe he'll be interested in investing if we get on his good side."

Teodulfo can get a cat on a dog's good side," Isidro was confident. "Everything is going to work out fine."

The Three Amigos, as they were referred to by the Mexicans, arrived at the Corregidor at 6 PM that Saturday and were well-received by the Filipinos. Many of them had attended the card games and greatly enjoyed the men's night out it provided. Apolonio introduced them to Joe Doctor, a well-known figure throughout the community. He was a friendly man with a great personality who was known for helping out a friend in need. He hit it off immediately with Teodulfo, and they were deep in conversation when Apolonio took the floor.

"My friends, I'm glad everybody was able to come out tonight. As you know, we sent out an extra special invitation tonight to welcome a new friend to our community. Ladies and gentlemen, it is a great pleasure to introduce Mr. Toribio Rivera and his lovely wife Nora."

Teodulfo was thunderstruck as the middle-aged, debonair gentleman joined Apolonio in the middle of the floor. He waved and thanked everyone, then introduced his wife before thanking everyone for their hospitality. He could not believe he was looking at Nora Rivera, the girl of the same name they had left behind in the Philippines almost a year ago. She looked around the room and smiled at everyone, though glancing past Teodulfo and his friends as if they were not there.

"Holy smoke, Dulfo, do you see who that is?" Hercules sidled over to him at the bar.

"Shut the hell up," he insisted. "Don't either one of you go near her. If she comes over, fine, but just hang loose until I can figure this out."

"Yeah, well, I'll go tell the other genius, and maybe he can help you figure this out. I'll see you tomorrow at your place."

"Tomorrow?"

"I'm out of here. You're on your own."

Teodulfo watched as Hercules walked over to where Isidro sat with a couple of other men in a far corner. They exchanged words before Hercules made his exit, Isidro wearing his usual poker face as he returned to his conversation. He could see that he was going to be the one to sort this out, and someone was going to have to do it soon before it exploded in their faces. Only he realized he was the one who would bear the brunt of the blast.

Although he continued getting to know Joe Doctor, he was as a cat watching the surroundings while listening to Joe's stories. He watched as the couple was given seats at a decorated table in the far corner opposite from where Isidro sat. He watched as Isidro fidgeted and squirmed, then finally came over and told Teodulfo he had an appointment. Teodulfo merely sat and smiled, realizing they had left him holding the bag.

Finally he saw Nora Rivera leave her seat and head to the outhouse on the patio. He waited until she had crossed the floor in the rear seating area before excusing himself to Joe. He looked about furtively, making sure that no one else was heading in that direction before walking across towards the rear exit.

"Nora?"

She stopped suddenly as he called to her across the patio, and he thought he saw her shoulders stiffen. He walked over to her, and she turned around with her eyes widened though her face appeared strangely impassive. He sensed that she was probably feeling as emotional as he was, but the awkwardness was shattered as she hauled off and slapped him as hard as she could across the face.

"You shitheel!" she blazed. "You lousy rotten shitheel! You lousy bastards ran off and left me back on the Islands without even saying goodbye!"

"Nora, I can explain."

"Don't even try, you little bastard! You owe me, you son of a bitch, you owe me! I had to get married and leave my family to come over here! We were a team, and the three of you turned your backs on me and left me behind!"

"We didn't have a choice. We had a chance and we took it. I never even got to say goodbye to my family. I would have gotten in touch with you eventually, you know that."

"It's too late now!"

"It's never too late."

"You little shitheel!" she cried, hauling off and slapping him once more with all her might across the face. She whirled and disappeared into the outhouse just as the door opened and closed behind him.

"Teodulfo," Apolonio came over. "Is everything okay?"

"Just fine," Teodulfo assured him. "I thought I recognized Mrs. Rivera from the Islands. You know, back in Manila."

"So you know each other." They both knew Apolonio could not have missed the redness on his face.

"Yes, we do. Say, uh, do you think we could..."

"It's fine, my friend, I just came to use the toilet, take care of business, you know."

"Sure, sure."

"Just as I know you will take care of your own business," Apolonio said pointedly, patting him on the shoulder before he walked past and stepped into the men's outhouse. Teodulfo headed back to the club, not feeling as if he needed to use the toilet at all.

Chapter Seven

Teodulfo David Dizon Jr. was born to Stella and Teodulfo on June of 1919. He was a healthy and vociferous baby, reminding one and all when he was and wasn't in the room during every waking hour. Stella's sisters were constantly stopping by to coddle the baby, and Teodulfo mildly complained that he wasn't even given time to carry his own child at times. His in-laws soon convinced him that it was the natural order of things.

"I don't think I got to spend time with my boy until he got old enough to shave," John Munoz kidded him. "Of course, they didn't have a clue, so they had no alternative."

By that time, all three of the Munoz brothers had gotten married though they had no intentions of settling down just yet. They had connections in Nuevo Laredo who were able to bring marijuana across the border. Though it was a risky business, they had gotten to where they were selling the product in small quantities and making extra money to feed their families. Although Teodulfo and Isidro refused to get involved with drugs, Hercules was setting his own gambling winnings aside and now had even more money to party with.

"Why don't you invest more of that money in the lending business?" Isidro would badger Hercules when they got together in the Bicals' back yard underneath Teodulfo's slowly-spreading pecan tree. "We've barely got enough to move around these days, and it's much safer than that locoweed you fellows are messing with. Mind you, it's much more risky than lending money. If the police start snooping around, they're liable to send you home. You know we still don't even have our citizenship papers yet."

"You should talk," Hercules scoffed. "You think I don't know anything about those opium dens the Chinese are running off Broadway? Word travels fast along the underworld, my friend. They are making money you have no idea of. You are being kept out of the inner circle. Believe me, your Mr. Wong has a lot more going than lending money. If he let you invest in some of those products, you would be owning your own restaurant and laundry in a very short time, my friend."

"I am warning you," Isidro shook a finger at him. "You are the one who is sticking your neck out. I don't know everything I should about the way things are done in this country, but I know this. The police may look the other way when they smell burning rope in your little *barrios*, but opium is considered narcotics. People who get caught dealing in narcotics are either thrown into prison or out of the country, never to return. I don't know about you, but I enjoy living in this country too much to take that chance."

"And what about you, Mr. Opinion?" Hercules chided Teodulfo. "You have nothing to say about this matter? Here you are with a wife and child, surely you'll be looking for a bigger house when your second child comes along. You owe me a godson, you know. You put Apolonio in a place of honor in all things, but I'll do him in if you try and make him godfather of your next one."

"Get lost, you big lout," Teodulfo blew him off. "You know it's all politics. Of course I'll have you stand for the next one, and Isidro for the one after that. After all, he was the one who sponsored us in the community. We wouldn't be doing nearly as well as we are if it wasn't for him."

"Speak for yourself, mister," Hercules swigged his beer. "I've got the Mexicans and Isidro had his Chinamen. You're the one standing on shoulders there. Why, you've only got one game a week going with them. You could leave here tomorrow and not lose a step."

"Bear one thing in mind," Teodulfo reminded him. "When push comes to shove, people l side with their own. If politics ever change things, circles will begin closing. The Mexicans will stand with Mexicans, and the Chinese will side with Chinese. Fortunately for me, I'm married into them, but you fellows had best keep it in mind. They will cast you out. Make sure you've always got connections among your own people."

"They have no organization besides the Corregidor," Hercules grunted. "A little hole in the wall club is no organization."

"That will change, my friends," Teodulfo said cryptically. "That will change."

World War I had ended a few months earlier, and the newspapers were filled with headlines about how the Germans were being forced to accept the Treaty of Versailles. Enlisted men were coming home from Europe, and it was a festive occasion throughout San Antonio and its military facilities. Surplus goods were being made available in the commissaries, and the wholesale prices allowed for underground traders to make quick profits at resale. As a result, local economies were thriving and it seemed that happy days were here again.

Teodulfo was feeling as if on top of the world that Monday afternoon as he adjusted his tie, staring out the window at the traffic below on East Houston Street. He had been given time off that day as the Sibleys had gone out of town for a family occasion. He made some phone calls and arrangements, and it allowed him to spend an enjoyable afternoon at the prestigious Gunter Hotel.

"So when do I get to see you again?" Nora Rivera asked as she adjusted her garters, sitting on the king-sized bed in the luxurious boudoir.

"Well, it all depends when we can set something up," he turned to her. "You know it's pretty hectic with the baby, and all the business going on at the club. That husband of yours is quite an entrepreneur. They told me he's already closing the deal on his own general store on Military Drive. It's a darned good thing he didn't choose a place here downtown or on Broadway. It'd make it pretty hard for you to go sneaking around."

"Don't get condescending with me, mister," her eyes flashed at him. "I wouldn't be sneaking around if you hadn't snuck out on me."

"Let me ask you something. Why is it that no matter how good of a time we have together, you always find a way to end it on a sour note?"

"Quit acting stupid," she launched herself out of bed and began angrily brushing her long silken hair. "You get to go home to your wife and kid. I get to go home to the old man."

"You keep saying that, and you know what I'm going to say next."

"And you know what I'm going to say to that!" she whirled to face him. "You think I could've married some young guy who was going to bring me over here? You and those friends of yours are the only ones I've ever known who had the guts to leave everything behind. You took a gamble to come here with nothing, absolutely nothing. I'm a woman, I couldn't take that chance. I had to have someone to bring me here. I had no choice, none whatsoever."

"All right. We can't change what's happened, what's done is done. Let's just enjoy what we've got. You've got a swell house, after all, with an upstairs and downstairs. He's even got his own automobile. I'm riding a bicycle to work. Now he's got his own business. I'm working as a house boy for the Sibleys. You're so far ahead of the rest of us, it's not funny. You've got a wardrobe that makes the women at the club look like washerwomen. You should really take stock and count your blessings. Besides, you have to love him, after all he's give you."

"Of course I love him, and it's not like I don't appreciate it. I know he's given me everything, and I'll always love him for that. But it's not the same as falling in love. I need someone who makes me feel like I'm in love, not just loving someone. Oh, what's the use?"

"I know what you mean," he could no longer control himself, watching the emotions course through her lovely face, standing there in her lingerie. He walked over and took her in his arms.

"Let me go, you've had enough," she halfheartedly pushed him away.

"It's never enough," he insisted, pushing her back on the bed, where she no longer resisted.

* * *

There was a new project underway at the Corregidor Club, and two of the main advocates happened to be Teodulfo Bical and Toribio Rivera. They had envisioned something beyond the informal social club to bind the Filipino community together. They saw the American Legion and the Veterans of Foreign Wars organizations as a paradigm. The two ex-military groups were burgeoning with new members and had expanded their operations to humanitarian causes which earned them even greater support. Teodulfo wanted something for the Filipinos that catered to their needs and brought them closer as a distinct population.

"The Filipino-American Society?" Apolonio pondered as Teodulfo and Toribio brought the subject before the major figures at the Club at an informal meeting. "I suppose it could work. I just hope it doesn't attract too much attention. You know how the Anglos can be, especially with their military mentality. I haven't been gone from the Islands long enough to have forgotten how it can get. If they thought for one minute we were trying to turn this into a political movement, they could take steps to pressure us into closing down."

"That's crazy," Teodulfo insisted. "I don't even know what the Filipino flag looks like. Besides, how many of us are there, a couple hundred? Even if we did decide to become politically active, where would we stand? I wouldn't know what a Democrat or a Republican was if they walked in here with guns and demanded we took sides. All there was back home was the democracy and the rebels, and if you threw in with the rebels you'd better have been ready to move to the jungle. That political talk is for the birds. All this will amount to is a place where Filipinos can get together among their own kind."

"Well, since you put it that way," Apolonio concurred, his feathers slightly ruffled.

"Dulfo is right," Toribio was emphatic. "Anyone who accuses us of having ulterior motives can go jump in the lake. We should have a place where we can take joy in who we are. We can't join the veterans' organizations because none of us have been in the military. We have no fellowship with the Chinese, and why would we seek it? A Filipino-American Society is something we would build for our children, for the future of our community. If we get this going and strengthen it, it will thrive and prosper far beyond the walls of this little club."

"Well, that's just fine," Federico San Juan, the owner of the club, spoke up. "Use me as a springboard, why don't you?"

"Come on, my friend," Toribio chided him. "Would you limit the Society to your club? I'm sure you would want it to grow so we have many chapters one day, like the Anglo clubs."

"All right, then," he waved his hand. "Do as you will. Let us schedule a meeting and see how this thing is taken by our neighbors."

And so it was that the word was spread so that the Corregidor Club was packed to the max that Wednesday evening. Toribio had donated a dozen luncheon tables and six dozen folding chairs which were set up in the rear dining hall of the club. By the time the meeting was called to order at six that evening, men were lining the walls as all the seats were taken. Apolonio waved his hand before his face in distaste as cigarette smoke had engulfed the small, poorly-ventilated room.

"I am glad so many of you were able to take time to come out and support us this evening," he waited until the singsong chatter subsided. At least half of the attendees were speaking in their native Tagalog. "Fortunately most of you were able to speak to us individually about the Society, and everyone seems to agree with our goals. What we would like to do is elect officers who will make up a charter to be approved at the next meeting. At that time we will start making plans for our monthly get-together, which I am sure will be a great success."

"I would like to nominate Apolonio as our President," Teodulfo spoke up. "It goes without saying that he is a leader in our community and a true gentleman. I can't think of anyone who would better represent this organization."

"No, no, my friend," Apolonio shook his head as he, Teodulfo, Toribio, Isidro and Joe Doctor sat at the table at the front of the room. "I'm more than glad to support the Society in any way I can, but frankly I don't have the energy that this position deserves."

"Well, then," he was taken somewhat aback, "obviously this honor should then fall upon our friend Toribio, who has so generously donated all these tables and chairs, as well as his good name and reputation to our cause."

"Afraid not, my young friend," Toribio declined. "I've got more than enough to preoccupy my time, what with my new business and my pretty young wife to tend to."

"Don't even look here, fellow," Joe Doctor arched an eyebrow.

"That makes it unanimous," Isidro called out to the crowd. "I nominate Teodulfo Bical as our new President."

He was about to deliver his rebuttal, but was drowned out by the cheers and yells from the boisterous gathering. Federico announced that he had tapped a keg for the members to enjoy free of charge in honor of the occasion. Everyone began gathering around as glasses were being passed out, leaving a bemused Teodulfo at the table as the first President of the Filipino-American Society of San Antonio, Texas.

Isidro was named the Society's adjutant by default, and he dutifully added the position to his growing list of responsibilities behind the scenes. Only more pressing matters were requiring his attention, and he saw no alternative to turn to his friends for help.

"Did you ever hear of the Chinese Tong?" Isidro asked them as they met at his apartment the next evening.

"Is that what they call those sticks they eat with?" Hercules furrowed his brow.

"It's a gang that came over here from China," Isidro explained. "There seems to be quite a few of them relocating from San Francisco. It's been going on for quite a while, but now they're approaching the Chinese business owners here in this area. Mr. Wong has been putting them off, but they're getting too persistent and he's asking that we come out to meet with them."

"Now what good are we going to do at a meeting between Chinamen?" Teodulfo asked. "And besides, I don't think it's a good idea for us to be getting involved with gangs."

"Don't you think that's coming a little late?" Hercules smirked.

"Look, your business with my brothers-in-law is your business, just like Isidro's business with the Chinese is his affair. I've got a wife and a kid, and besides, I'm not exactly the type who goes about getting in street brawls over territories and money-making schemes."

"Do I look like I'm going to the table with a blackjack in my pocket?" Isidro retorted. "What Mr. Wong wants is to have a show of solidarity with other groups in the community. The Tong's influence comes from their ability to prey upon their own people, making them feel isolated and dependent on their own group. If they see that Mr. Wong's interests extend beyond the Chinese, it may cause the Tong to become discouraged."

"Wong Tong, Tong Wong," Hercules poked fun at him. "Go ahead and set it up. I don't intend to get in the middle of an argument between Chinese, but I certainly don't want our well to dry up either."

The group of eight awaited their visitors at the Szechuan Empire the next evening. The Three Amigos arrived along with Celestino, and they were introduced to Mr. Wong and three of his associates. The members of the Chinese Tong arrived at 6 PM sharp, and they were escorted to a private room in the rear of the restaurant. One of Mr. Wong's friends acted as an interpreter, and he only passed along what pertained to them despite the fact both sides were jabbering intently in their native Cantonese.

"They're saying that Wong is disrespecting the traditions of his ancestors in dealing outside the Chinese community," the Chinaman explained as the conversation grew particularly animated. "Foreigners engaging with Chinese see them as second-class citizens and will inevitably short-change them at some point. It places all Chinese at risk in making them seem weak and gullible. They insist that Wong restrict his activities to our community so that we all grown strong together."

"That's hypocrisy," Teodulfo insisted. "What is he supposed to do, close his doors to Americans and fellow immigrants? It would cut his business in half and he'd end up closing his doors. That's one less Chinese-owned business in the community."

The interpreter passed along the comment and was met with angry resistance from the Tong members.

"They say the Filipinos and the Mexicans are no different than the rest. The Filipinos are from the same side of the ocean as us but pledge allegiance to money. They say the Mexicans who cross the border into America also believe in nothing but money."

"So maybe they can tell us what the hell they are here for, if not for money?" Hercules snarled."

"There should be no reason why all cannot share and contribute to one another's successes," Isidro added. "After all, we all came here to realize our dreams. Thieves and robbers operate in the darkness. All the men at this table have come of their own accord, with nothing to hide and to declare our good intentions."

The Tong members made some closing remarks, then stood up and walked out without farewells or shaking hands.

"They said they will wait and see. They told Mr. Wong they hoped he would not regret his decision."

Teodulfo and his friends departed shortly afterward. They felt as if they had resolved whatever issues there were, but had little doubt they had not heard the last of the Chinese Tong.

Chapter Eight

By May of 1921, Manuel Amador was born to Stella and Teodulfo.

Teodulfo not only made Hercules the baby's godfather but named him after Emmanuel Luzon, which was Hercules' real name. Hercules felt greatly honored, and Isidro was assured he would be the godfather of their next child. The baptism party was held at the Corregidor Club, and the next two gatherings at the Bical home and the Welks were elaborate affairs in honor of the newest addition to the family.

"You know, family's the most important thing," Ed Welk emphasized after taking Teodulfo aside during the get-together at his home on Hays Street. "My family's spread over the Dakotas and along the West Coast. I guess you know about me being a second cousin to Lawrence Welk. Well, me and him are about as close as the tips on a longhorn steer. Same as the rest of the family. When I came down here and got hooked up with Charlotte, it was the first time I really got to see what family was about. They took me in even though I was a big old German fellow with nothing in common with them. I got to meet her sisters and brothers, all their cousins, nieces and nephews, and the family keeps growing all the time."

"I know the feeling," Teodulfo sympathized as they sat in a corner of Ed's spacious backyard as the family gathered around the luncheon table and its scrumptious spread of Mexican food. "I left my whole family behind back in San Pedro. I never even had a chance to say goodbye to my parents. The Colonel I was working for gave me a one-time-only offer, and I didn't dare pass it up."

"See, that's the problem," Ed growled. "Those sons of bitches could've handled it a lot better than that. He could've let you tie up your loose ends and sent for you afterwards, especially a shitbird Colonel. They just do everything for their own convenience, see how high they can make other men jump. He wanted to show everyone Stateside all the servants he had at his beck and call. Now, you got a good thing going here, and I don't want you to mess it up by holding anything against Sibley. I guess you should be thankful things worked out the way they did. You would've never met that little girl and got married, had those two boys or ended up with a brother-in-law like me."

"No, I certainly don't hold anything against the Colonel, no sir," Teodulfo replied. I agree that meeting him was the greatest thing that ever happened to me. Well, except for meeting Stella, but you're right, it couldn't have happened without the Colonel. Maybe it could've been handled differently. But, by golly, I'm putting money together little and little, and one day I'm going to introduce my wife and sons to my Mom, you can bet on it."

His business associates did not doubt his resolve, and in fact were optimistic about his chances, considering how well they were doing on the street.

"You know, I don't see why you couldn't pull this trip of yours off for about a grand," John Munoz considered as he studied his poker hand at the five-man game beneath the shade of a pecan tree. "Four people, hotel expenses, travel costs and all, it's doable. You've achieved every goal you set out to reach since you been here. Hell, you ran off with my baby sister and lived to tell of it."

"Nah, you know he would've had me to hide behind," Hercules puffed smoke from his cigar as he threw a dollar into the pot.

"That's what I like about this guy," Pete Munoz chuckled. "If you listen to him, you'd think they could've won at the Alamo by having him beat down all the Mexicans."

"Not all," Hercules decided. "Some. Well, most."

"*Finche cabron*," Dave Munoz laughed, swigging a beer. "If only he realized how tough all those switchblades behind him really makes him."

"Yeah, hiding behind me about a block away," Hercules shot back before tossing down a full house and raking in the pot.

"He gets any luckier, he won't need anyone behind him," Isidro pulled a five-dollar bill from his wallet. He decided to take a break from the game and joined Teodulfo for a walk outside.

"The newspapers are talking about a Depression that's been going on in this country since last year," Teodulfo was concerned. "President Harding says it's almost over, but what about our money? If the banks go under, can we lose everything?"

"There's not a whole lot of our money in the banks," Isidro revealed. "Most of our money is on the street. If the street collapses along with the economy, then we are in trouble. But I can fairly well assure you, the street will never collapse. Even if the Government collapses, the street will never collapse."

Teodulfo found that he was not the only one concerned about the state of the underground economy. He had just about completed his daily chores that Monday afternoon when Colonel Sibley invited him to sit with him in the gazebo in his spacious back yard. He asked Teodulfo to bring two tall glasses of iced tea and cookies which he himself had baked.

"We haven't had a chance to talk for a while," the Colonel was pleasant. "How are things at home, now that you've got another little fellow at the house?"

"Well, it's keeping the wife busy but I think little Dolfo is enjoying having a little brother around. I consider it a blessing when I think about being all alone here with my friends less than four years ago. I owe it all to you, Colonel, and I'll never forget that."

"Dulfo, you're a hard worker and you deserve everything you have. I'm proud to be able to say I brought you over. You know, it's a good thing that you seized the opportunity to make the move. Just between you and me, there's a lot of talk going on about a new Act of Congress that may be closing the doors entirely by 1924."

"Gee, I didn't know anything about that."

"You see, what's happening is that people in high places have been seriously discussing the need to preserve the ideal of American homogeneity. It goes without saying that we are a nation of immigrants, but keep in mind that our country was founded by white Anglo-Saxon Protestants. We are descendants of the English people, just as they are descendants of the white Israelites under the Covenant of Abraham. I don't want to overburden you with these ponderous concepts. What it boils down to is that we cannot afford to allow the peoples of the earth to flood our nation and dilute its ethnicity down to some generic proportion. Do you understand what I'm saying?"

"I think so. I know you remember how it was back in the Philippines. They were always worried that the Chinese might try and take over if more and more of their people migrated."

"Yes, the Chinese," Sibley nodded sagely. "Some say they multiply like cockroaches. They are flooding our harbors in California, and together with the Japanese they're making it difficult to keep the doors open for noble people like the Filipinos. I'm sure you can see the need to keep an eye on these fellows, can't you?"

"I'm sure I can."

"Lots of the senior officers at Fort Sam are concerned that the criminal element within the Chinese community may be posing a threat to our own neighborhoods," Sibley revealed. "Some of our men in uniform have been overheard complaining about being overwhelmed by debt incurred by loans they've taken from the Chinese. Lots of these loans were taken out as a result of their addiction to gambling and drugs. I'm sure you know who provides the outlets for drugs and gambling."

"I can see where this could be a problem."

"I'm sure. I know your friend Isidro has a job with the Chinese, and your friend Hercules rubs elbows with Chinese in his travels as a landscaper. See if they can keep you informed. If they hear of any suspicious activity, let me know. The officers at Fort Sam are working closely with the San Antonio Police Department to keep our streets safe and secure. We want to make sure that the Chinese don't get out of control. We know that we can't eliminate crime entirely, but drugs is something we will never tolerate."

"You can rely on me, Colonel. I've got my ear to the ground. You can be sure that my friends and I are doing everything we can to be outstanding American citizens."

"So what is it are you complaining about? You've heard that old saying, you can't have your cake and eat it too."

"Well, sometimes you can come close."

"Like you're doing right now, huh?"

Nora Rivera looked over at Teodulfo as he sat at the window of their suite at the Gunter Hotel late that Tuesday afternoon. He had gotten into a routine of taking the bus downtown and meeting Nora on Tuesdays and Thursdays, telling Stella that he was delivering messages to the Colonel's stockbrokers. He would get home after dark, which was not overly late and gave him enough time to keep Nora happy. She, in turn, was asked no questions by Toribio. The old man made it a top priority to keep his young wife content.

"Come on, it's hard enough without having to sit around and talk about it."

"You're the one who brought up your friends. You can talk about their problems, but you can't talk about mine."

"You don't have a problem. Hercules is out on the street collecting money and running muscle for the Mexicans. Who knows what Isidro's involved in. They don't realize what's going on. That's all we heard back home, the Americans will do this and that. It was water off the duck's back. In this situation, we can be thrown out of the country, never to return. There's no protection from that. Isidro's the smarter of the two, and he won't listen to me. He thinks Sibley just called me aside to spread a rumor that the officers at the Fort want people to hear."

"You always say he's the smartest one of the three of you. You should listen to him."

"I said he's good with numbers. I'm the one who puts everything together. Don't try and tick me off."

"You're ticked off before you even walk in here. You can't even get it up half the time."

"I think you're oversexed. You ought to try feeding your husband oysters, or put some of those Chinese potions in his food."

"I thought I told you to keep my husband out of this."

"Sure, everything else is fair game for you. You can make these little digs about my friends, or ask questions about my family, but your sugar daddy is off-limits."

"What did you just say?" she flared up, stopping in the middle of her room-delivered supper. Teodulfo had not touched his plate.

"You know, I've got enough trash to take out, I don't need yours," he stormed over and yanked his jacket off the coat rack. "I've got things to take care of, I'm not going to be able to make it Thursday."

"Suit yourself," she concealed her disappointment. "The room's paid for the rest of the year. Toribio's getting a tax write-off for the business expense. It's supposed to be for out-of-town guests."

"Good. You can bring him up here."

"You'll be back," she lazily extended her black-stockinged leg. She had gained ten pounds since she came to the States, and the extra weight had made her voluptuous.

"Yeah, well, don't hold your breath," he shot back before slamming the door behind him.

The Bicals had been invited to John Munoz' home that Saturday for a celebration of the third birthday of John Junior. Stella had brought Dolfo and Manuel earlier that afternoon, and Teodulfo rode his bike to their home on Muncey Street after work. Hercules and Isidro were attending the weekly gathering at the Corregidor Club, and sent word they would catch up with him at his home on Sunday.

The place was crowded as usual, and Teodulfo made the rounds in greeting all the family members who were already there. He gave John Jr. a dollar, then thanked Maria Munoz for a bottle of Coke. He then accompanied Pete out to the back where John and Dave awaited at a rear table. They seemed somewhat reserved as they greeted Teodulfo, and there was an unusual silence before they started exchanging pleasantries.

"You know, the cops have been coming around," John said tersely as he took a swig of beer. "Has Hercules mentioned anything to you?"

"No, we've got an agreement," Teodulfo replied. "I don't really want to know about his business with you, it's none of my affair. You're family, he's my friend, and we leave it at that."

"He said something about that Army guy you work for saying some stuff," Dave mentioned. "Something about them looking at the Chinese."

"That stuff's in the newspapers. The Government's talking about limiting immigration in the next year or so. I read that they've got too many Jews in New York coming over from Eastern Europe."

"We don't live in New York, *carnal*. We're in San Antone," John pointed out. "The problem here is the Chinese coming from California. You see, the *bolillos*[1] don't have a problem with Mexicans, they stole this land from us.

"We got a problem with them. The problem they got is with Chinese. They ain't never gonna close the border with Mexico, but they sure will keep those Chinese out if they think they need to."

"So it looks like all this stuff with the Government and the military and the police won't affect us—or you—or whoever."

"You're family," Pete reminded him. "Us is you. Don't forget that. You're married to our sister. You're the father of our nephews. Our mother is your children's *abuela*. Don't forget that. Blood is thicker than water. Those children are half Dizon, or Bical, or whatever you call yourself, but they're also half Munoz."

"I don't get where you're coming from," Teodulfo furrowed his brow. "What are you trying to say? Am I missing something here?"

"We know you've been screwing around on my sister," John stared at him. "I got people downtown, they see you. I got no problem with that, I screw around on my wife all the time. You just make sure it don't do anything that hurts the family. If she leaves you, and she takes the kids, you can't stop her. You should be aware of that."

"Hey, wait a second," Teodulfo leaned back in his seat. "Let's slow this down."

"That discussion's over," John said flatly. "That's all I got to say on it. What we need to talk about is your friend Isidro. I know he's managing money for the Chinese, and I know you and Hercules have been investing with them. You see, when the police want to find out how a racket gets set up, they follow the

---

1. white bread

money trail. If they want to close down the drugs or the moneylending, they follow the money. What me and my brothers do here is what the cops call nickel-and-dime. We ain't shit. If they want us to back up, they just take one of us downtown and kick the shit out of us."

"You can't do that with the Chinese because they do everything behind closed doors," Pete chimed in. "The cops need warrants to go in after them. It's too much trouble. For that kind of stuff, they go for the throat. If they go through the trouble of getting a warrant, somebody's going away for a very long time. In the case of an immigrant, he gets thrown out and he can never come back."

"I'm not making a connection here."

"They're asking about Isidro. Apparently Hercules doesn't know anything about it, and that's why we're coming to you. You need to tell Isidro to break it off with the Chinese quick, or something's gonna happen."

"He's got a legitimate job with them, and he's making good money. How can you ask me something like that?"

"Listen, *hermano*, this is big," Dave admonished him. "Bigger than anything we've seen. We think it's about the Chinese Tong. They're supposed to be one of the biggest gangs in the world, bigger than anything we got in Mexico. They say there's an Italian gang in New York called the Mafia *tambien*. The *bolillos* think that if they join forces, they may be able to overthrow the government, like in Russia. They ain't gonna let that happen. *Carnal*, you need to move Isidro out the way, because the storm is coming."

Teodulfo had no way of knowing just how soon the storm would arrive.

"*Que paso?*"

Teodulfo nearly jumped out of bed as Stella pulled away from him, sitting up in alarm at the pounding at the door. They heard

Manuel crying in the cradle near the foot of the bed, and Dolfo calling for his mother from the next room.

"I'll see who it is. You get the baby."

Teodulfo crept to the door and peeked to the shutters, taken aback by the sight of Hercules at the doorstep.

"What in heck is going on?" he demanded, looking to see if his neighbors' lights had come on. "Do you know what time it is?"

"It's Isidro," he seemed almost as if dazed. "The *migra*[2] came for him. I tried to see what I could do but they started acting like they were gonna mess me up next. I went to John and the son of a bitch turned his back on me. I don't have a clue as to how to contact the Chinese."

"The *migra*?" Teodulfo grew ashen. "We don't even have our green cards yet. What the heck are they after him for?"

"As far as I know, it had something to do with the Chinese Tong. I went straight downtown after they took him away, and they already knew who I was. They had a file on me, they knew I'm with the Munozes. They told me they weren't interested in me, but they could be if I didn't mind my own business."

"Where did they take him?"

"I'm pretty sure they're taking him back to San Francisco."

As it turned out, the Treasury Department under auspices of the Commissioner of Immigration was coordinating efforts with the Department of Justice. Their objective was to sever links between the criminal underworld and local immigrant communities as a preemptive action. It would eventually precipitate the passage of the Immigration Act of 1924. The Chinese Tong was identified as a potential threat in major Southwest cities, and Federal agents were working with local authorities to build dossiers on suspected Tong affiliates.

---

2. Immigration

The Chinese gang acted swiftly to sever their connections with the outside world. They met with Mr. Wong and advised him that he would have to sacrifice Isidro as part of a deal they made with the Feds. They were going to lie low and curtail their own drug-dealing, gambling and moneylending enterprises. Wong would have to do the same. They had already given Isidro's name to the Feds, and after he was arrested and things cooled off, things would go back to normal. Only the business between the Mexicans and the Chinese would come to an end.

Isidro had met Hercules after work and was going to stop by the Szechuan Empire to touch bases with Wong. Only they saw the police cars parked outside the restaurant and suspected something was amiss. They started back in the opposite direction but were cut off by an unmarked car, whose occupants ushered them inside. They were taken downtown to the Bexar County Jail, where they were fingerprinted and taken away for questioning.

There was no question-and-answer session. Isidro was told he had violated his agreement with the Government in engaging in questionable activity as an immigrant to the US. Since he was not a naturalized citizen, Texas had no jurisdiction. He would be returned to California where they would review his application for citizenship.

Neither Teodulfo nor Hercules would ever hear from Isidro again.

Chapter Nine

Daniel David was born to Stella and Teodulfo in June of 1923, given his godfather Dave's name as his baptismal name. By now Gilberto and Beatrice had their own family started, and Sara and Gilbert Jr. were in the backyard playing with their cousins daily. Though the sisters were very close, Gilbert was a workaholic who was determined to avoid involvement in the business of his brothers. As a result, he and Teodulfo were friendly but never grew intimate.

Teodulfo had a phone installed that summer, and it proved to be a bigger hindrance than he anticipated. Stella's sisters badgered their husbands to follow suit, and soon she was on the phone chatting with them throughout each day. When she got off the phone, he would be getting calls from members of the Filipino-American Society about upcoming events, or Hercules touching bases over some piddling matter. He soon realized that it was Hercules' way of filling the void in his life left by Isidro. Only Teodulfo was starting to feel as if he didn't have a life of his own.

He would grow distracted by thoughts of his family back home, wondering if Isidro had contacted them and told them what had become of the Three Amigos. He was fairly certain that Isidro would have given them his address. He wondered if his father had forbade the family to make contact with him. He knew he had always been contentious with his brothers, yet it would seem unlikely that they would cut him off entirely. Still, who could tell? He knew his father and brothers were all proud men, and their feelings might have been badly hurt by knowing Teodulfo had left the Islands without even saying goodbye. Even worse, it might have been more about the grief it caused his mother than anything else.

"Am I ever going to meet my grandmothers?" Dolfo asked as the two of them sat in the backyard one evening, gazing at the stars.

"I don't see why not," Teodulfo replied.

He was experiencing growing pains as his family grew larger. He saw that the Mexicans seemed to go from one extreme to the other in relating to their children. It was the carrot and the stick, they would spoil them one minute and beat the heck out of them the next. He would look back at his parents and often tried to think of how his father would have handled things. Only when he did so, he came across too strict and would cause Stella to feel bad. Dolfo always seemed to be left out of sorts, and Teodulfo felt guilty because of it.

"Do you think I'll go to the moon one day?"

"Maybe. They're making movies about going to the moon. I don't see why they won't just go ahead and do it one day."

"I want to go to the moon, Daddy."

"Well, if you do well in school, you never know. Maybe you won't get to go, but maybe you'll help somebody else get there."

"Wow. That would be great."

"Yep. I never dreamed I'd be here in America. You just have to follow your dreams, boy."

"I want to visit my Grandma Cytherea and my Grandpa Adonis, and all my uncles. I'm going to take them to the moon with me."

"You just make sure you tell your Mom before you go," he felt a lump grow in his throat. As an afterthought, he pulled Dolfo into his lap. The little boy was delighted by the unusual display of affection, and laid his head back against his father's shoulder.

"Do you think they'll like me?" he asked softly.

"Of course they'll like you. They'll love you. You're their blood. And blood is thicker than water."

"I love you, Daddy."

"Be quiet," Teodulfo wiped a tear from his eye. "Let's just imagine being on the moon."

A short time later, he carried his peacefully sleeping son back into the house.

The Government's agenda became evident as 1924 grew near. The proposed Immigration Act would come hand and hand with the National Origins Act and the Asian Exclusion Act. Their objective was to curtail the arrival of non-whites upon American shores, though there were a number of arbitrary exceptions available. Those skilled in the agriculture industry were eligible for exemption, which left the doors open for hundreds of thousands of migrant farm workers from Latin America. It would also be recorded that migration from the UK dropped by nineteen percent, while Italians and Jews found it nearly impossible to gain entry. Orientals arriving on the West Coast also found themselves barred from the US.

As a result, Colonel Sibley made an appointment to speed up the process in getting Teodulfo his green card. He was not about to take a chance in losing his loyal and most dependable house boy. They arrived at the offices of the INS on a Monday morning, and though the agents seemed reluctant to jump an applicant ahead of the pack, a few phone calls assured them that the Colonel had some political clout behind him.

"You know, Colonel, our purpose is not to discriminate against any particular race, creed or color," the agent informed them as they sat before his desk in the small but comfortable office. "Our biggest problem is the crime problem that is plaguing the nation. As you know, J. Edgar Hoover has been nominated to head a Federal agency dedicated to eliminating organized crime in this country. Most of the organized gangs are composed of Italians and Jews, but we also have more than our share of Chinese."

"You can see from the application that my man here is not Chinese," Sibley was gruff. "I brought him over from the Philippines. He's been here five years, and he's got a wife and family. Plus he's been working for me all this time, and he will continue to do so."

"We just want to make sure that he has no direct connections to any of these undesirable elements. We're most concerned with the On Leone Tong, who we know is operating here in San Antone. There's a major gang war going on in New York between them and the Hip Sing Tong, and we will be damned if we allow it to spread here. Those gangs earn millions of dollars from illegal enterprises, which makes them just as dangerous at the Mafia."

"I'm just as aware of the problem as you are. I personally could care less if they allow another chink, wop or kike into this country until hell freezes over. What I'm telling you is that my boy is all right. I brought him over here, he's been working for me ever since, and he'll be working for me until the day he dies. Now, I'm a full-bird Colonel, I served in the Philippines during the Spanish-American War. I thought this thing was settled. If I got to go out and climb up a tree to get this done, let me tell you, someone up there is gonna come down here and take a big dump on your desk before it's over."

"Look, Colonel, it's my job to make you aware about what's going on. I know one of his friends were sent back to San Francisco over alleged involvement with the Tongs. I'll go ahead and put this through, but you make sure your boy keeps his nose clean."

"Well, I was the one who brought that boy Isidro over, and I never even got a courtesy call about it. It damn sure better not happen with this boy."

"All right," the agent conceded. "Mr. Bical, you'll be contacted within thirty days."

"You want to do *what*?"

"Look, I got it straight from the horse's mouth. The door is closing next year, no one gets in. They told me outright that the Tong is worth millions. If we can get back in with Mr. Wong, we can double our money and get back out. I'll step into Isidro's place, and with my green card they can't just send me back to San Francisco. Sibley will bail me out. The whole world's going upside down next year with that Immigration Act. Who knows if they'll come after the Mexicans next? You don't know what can happen. You don't have your card, they can come after you. We should have enough, have connections so that you can disappear. Once you get your card, whatever we make will be free and clear. Let's take what we can before they close the Chinese down."

"Damn," Hercules shook his head as they sat in Teodulfo's yard that night after dinner. "You gonna risk the whole thing, everything, by going over to Wong's?"

"We could lose everything just as quick. We never even got to say goodbye to Isidro. The Government just took him away, just like that. It's no different than it was back home, don't you remember what it was like? The Government went into the *barrios*, the jungles, looking for someone, and when they found them you never heard of them again. How many of your relatives did you lose? How many people just disappeared? I don't want you disappearing on me. If they come for you, we'll have enough so you can get away, down to Mexico. You can stay down there until it gets right again."

"Why would you take a chance like this for me?"

"You're the only brother I got left. My family's turned their back on me, I know that. Isidro would've given them my address. I couldn't take it if I wrote them and got no response. You're all I got left, brother."

"Okay, let's do it."

They ushered Dolfo and Manuel back into the house as Teodulfo told Stella they would be going out for a little while.

"You're the godfather to my little boy, Emmanuel," she said softly as he kissed her cheek.

"I know that. Why do you say that?"

"I know where you're going, I know what you're up to."

"What?"

"C'mon," Teodulfo insisted. "Let's go."

"What the hell was that about?" Hercules grunted as he backed his Model-T Ford out of the narrow driveway.

"Those darned gossips in her family. They heard stories about somebody seeing me at that hotel downtown where Toribio keeps that guest room. They put two and two together and started a rumor."

"You don't mean you're still messing around with Nora."

"Of course not, I broke that off months ago. I told you that. Besides, if it ever got back to the old man, it'd ruin the Society. There's no way I'd ever let that happen."

"You and that damn Society. I hope you never have to choose between them and your family."

"Hey, that's no contest. My family comes first. That Society, though—that's my legacy in this community. Besides my sons, that's what I leave behind."

"Yeah, well," Hercules sniffed. "Let's hope you don't leave them too far behind."

Teodulfo would come to remember those words for a long, long time.

When Teodulfo returned that evening, he was in such a good mood that Stella decided enough was enough. She made some calls the next day and made plans to bring this situation to an end.

Her brothers had found out that the woman who frequented the Gunter Hotel was Nora Rivera, the wife of old Toribio from the Corregidor Club. They found out that she had known Teodulfo and his friends from the Philippines. The story was that they had worked together in Manila and she and Teodulfo were seeing each other. It was also said that she had been left behind when the Three Amigos came over, and she married the old man just to make it over here. She remembered meeting Nora and Toribio, but Teodulfo never let on. It was just like they said, he was a darned good poker player.

She sat at the bus stop for the entire morning, right across the street from the main entrance to the Gunter Hotel. She had left the boys with Beatrice next door, telling her she had an appointment downtown that would take up most of the day. Her sister thought it odd as Stella was a stay-at-home type, especially since the boys came along. Even so, she asked no questions as her youngest sister had been there for her through thick and thin. The Bicals had put food on their table more than a couple of times, and Beatrice would never forget it.

Stella often wondered if the spark was gone from their marriage. She had put on over twenty pounds since Dolfo was born, and her sisters would good-naturedly tease her that she looked like a little heifer. She was still as pretty as ever, and she always attracted whistles and propositions whenever she came downtown by herself. Their sex life was still healthy, yet she began wondering whether he had lost his desire. Sometimes he acted as if he was just going through the motions, or as if he was just trying to please her. Now she knew why.

She spotted Nora Rivera coming out of the hotel at about 3 PM. Nora was dressed to the max and had apparently gone to the beauty parlor, which filled Stella with a grudging anger. She saw the bus up the street and got up from the bench, retreating towards a store window so as to be unnoticeable on the busy street. Apparently Nora was in a hurry as she paid no mind to anyone, stepping in line behind other passengers boarding the Hays Street bus. Stella waited until Nora stepped up into the bus before she got in line behind the other riders.

Nora found herself an outside seat near the aisle, placing her handbag across her lap as she pulled out a kerchief and daubed her neck. It was almost ninety degrees outside and all the windows were wide open, allowing humid air to blow in. She grew annoyed at having waited a couple of minutes too long and missed the less-crowded 2:30 bus. She looked up in irritation at the front of the bus, and reacted much too slowly by the time Stella Bical reached her.

Stella grabbed two fistfuls of her hair and dragged her out into the aisle. Onlookers gasped in shock as she began hauling off, holding Nora's hair in one hand while hammering her with her right fist. Women began crying out as a couple of men made their way over but dared not intervene. Finally the bus driver shoved him way down the aisle and grabbed Stella's arms from behind. He pulled her away as Nora sank to the floor, Stella still holding large fistfuls of hair. Just before the driver pulled her off, she lunged forth and kicked Nora as hard as she could between the legs.

News spread like wildfire back to the neighborhood, and by the time Teodulfo got off work everyone knew what happened. Celestino was waiting at the south gate of Fort Sam, and there he gave Teodulfo the bad news. Teodulfo was as a condemned man as he mechanically pedaled across the bridge to Burleson Street. He slowly cruised up Can't Stop, and was somewhat relieved when he arrived. He found a note from Stella saying she was next door with the boys and would be home later.

It was after dark when he heard a knock on the door, and turned down the radio as he got up to see who it was. He answered the door and felt sick when he saw a police officer in the threshold.

"Oh, no," he raised a hand in apprehension. "Is this about my wife?"

"No, sir," the cop replied. "Do you know Emmanuel Luzon? We found your name and number in his wallet."

The meeting with Mr. Wong a few days ago had gone smoothly. Wong was glad to see the boys again and was happy to resume business. He regretted hearing about what happened to Isidro but was glad it was only a matter of being brought back to San Francisco. He was relieved that Isidro had not fallen victim to the On Leone Tong. The internecine war between the rival Tongs had escalated over the past few weeks, though the SAPD had kept the information from the press in order to keep the public from being alarmed.

Both Teodulfo and Hercules had brought $100 apiece, giving it to Mr. Wong as an investment in the moneylending venture. Wong was more than glad to accept the money, guaranteeing them the usual ten percent profit within a few weeks. He pointed out the fact that the military had cracked down on enlisted men getting involved in illegal activity, and had urged the SAPD to increase their undercover activities along Broadway as a result. Business was slow, but a couple of big loans would get things going again.

Unkonwn to Wong, the On Leone had some of their own people on the street. They found out that Wong had new money they were ready to lend, and decided that they would have to take measures to discourage any further transgressions. The Tong were fairly certain they had taken control of Broadway, and were not about to let Wong stage a comeback. Still, they knew Wong was being watched and could not take a chance in moving against him. It would give the SAPD the pretext that they needed to move in and crush the Chinese once and for all.

They reached out to one of their own Mexican connections who were trying to cut a deal with the Tong for an opium sale. The Texas Rangers were making it impossible to bring drugs in from Mexico, so opium was the next best option. The Tong leaders informed them that they were ready to negotiate, but they would need a favor in return. The Mexicans were overjoyed and informed the Tong they were more than willing to help.

Hercules had arrived at his apartment on East Grayson Street shortly before dark after a day of carousing with friends. He was feeling pretty good, and cursed and swore to find the bulb was missing in the hallway when he got home. He could barely see as he made his way to the staircase and pulled himself up the steps. He was going to have a word with the landlady about not even noticing the bulb was out.

He got to the top of the steps before he saw the figure standing at the next landing. He looked up and found himself staring into a double-barreled shotgun.

The gunman shot Emmanuel Luzon, native of the Philippine Islands, listed as a white male aged twenty-one, with both barrels in the face. He died instantly.

Chapter Ten

Their fourth son Frederick was born to Teodulfo and Stella in December of 1931. The stock market crash of 1929 had plunged the world into a Great Depression, and the minorities of San Antonio struggled more desperately than ever. Teodulfo's earnings at the Sibley home became a lifeline for the family, and he was forced to dig down ever deeper to help the Perez family next door as times got tougher.

Yet the family grew even more tightly knit as they drew together to make ends meet. Ed Welk stretched his military pension to the breaking point, buying sacks of rice, beans and flour for tortillas so that Charlotte always had food for relatives who came by. The Munoz brothers did likewise, continuing to cut corners on the street for whatever extra they could get. The Filipino-American Society became a pillar of the community, rallying support for the needy whenever possible. Fortunately there were so many from the Islands who had experienced such bitter poverty that they did not even consider the situation to be a hardship.

Teodulfo was somewhat grateful that Gilbert was spending time with Manuel and Daniel in the back yard. He had been a professional boxer and was teaching them the sweet science. Manuel grew highly proficient and learned tricks as quickly as Gilbert could teach them. Daniel was not as artistic and developed a more pugnacious style. As a result, they grew to complement each other's style and provided perfect sparring mates for one another. Gilbert would often compare the brothers to a matador and a bull as their sessions appeared almost as if choreographed to the casual observer.

Ed Welk would stop by and give the boys pointers, but the rugged German was so rough that Daniel would disappear when he showed up in the back yard. Manuel proved eager to learn whatever he could and took a couple of hammerings from Uncle Butch as a result. Yet it made him a better boxer and more impervious to punishment from bigger boys at the East Houston Boxing Club in years to come. Ed, in turn, developed an affinity for the gutsy boy and nicknamed him Stooge. It was a relationship they would nurture over a lifetime.

The family dynamics grew ever more challenging for Teodulfo as time went by. He was a small man at 5'6" and 120 pounds, never prone to violence or anger. Having to raise four spirited young boys proved daunting at times, and eventually he began ruling the home with an iron hand. Stella tended to rely on Manuel as the most responsible of the boys, while Teodulfo favored Daniel as the youngest son even after Fred came along. Dolfo seemed to have gotten overlooked, and he became reticent and withdrawn as a result. He began falling behind in his grades, and finally he was given the news that he was going to be left behind at school the following year if there was not a drastic improvement.

"So what are you going to do about this?" Teodulfo asked him as they had a father-son talk beneath the pecan tree one afternoon. "Do you mean to tell me you're going to let your younger brothers pass you by? Manuel comes home with all A's, and you're coming in with D's. Where's the pride? You're good at math, which is the hardest subject. Why not apply yourself to the other subjects the same way?"

"Well," Dolfo said sheepishly, "sometimes I just don't feel like it. Sometimes I feel like no one cares if I do well or not."

"Of course someone cares. Your mother cares and I care. Why, we named you after me, you're Dolfo Junior. Don't you feel proud of that?"

"Sure I do."

"Then you have to act like it. Don't you remember that time we sat out here, that night you said you were going to send someone to the moon one day? Did you give up on that?"

"No," Dolfo looked down, softly kicking at the grass with his shoe.

"Did you know that somebody from South Dakota, where Uncle Butch is from, invented something called the cyclotron the other day? It's an invention that will help scientists study nuclear physics. You know, if you did better in school, you could be a nuclear physicist someday. Wouldn't that be something? Can you imagine what my parents in the Philippines would think?"

"I bet they'd be proud," Dolfo's eyes lit up.

"Why, sure they'd be proud. And just think, when they read that you helped put someone on the moon, and saw your name was Dolfo Junior, don't you think that would make them twice as proud?"

"I bet they would be," Dolfo grinned.

"You go ahead and gather up some pecans, and I'll make us a nice big pie," Dolfo got up from his lawn chair and patted his son's head. "You just remember what we talked about. You make me proud, you hear? You're Dolfo Junior. Don't you forget that."

"I'm going to send a man to the moon one day!" he said gleefully.

"You sure will," Teodulfo smiled. "I know you will."

It was nearing Christmas of 1932, and the family had a get-together in honor of baby Freddie's first birthday. Shortly afterward, the Filipino-American Society announced that they would have a holiday celebration at the Corregidor Club. Nora and

Toribio Rivera had long since moved to Chicago, and the incident on the Houston Street bus a distant memory. Teodulfo had been the club president for over a decade, and no one would think of running against him. As a result, his wife and kids were treated like royalty when they graced the club with their presence.

"You know, people are going through a tough time right now with this Depression," Apolonio noted as he sat with Teodulfo at a table while the children marveled at the Christmas tree and all the presents beneath it. "People are always coming up and telling me how the Society has helped them get through this. We've made people feel special, like they're part of something great. If it wasn't for your vision, we would've never accomplished this."

"Don't give me all the credit," Teodulfo waved a hand. "You were the one who brought me in, made me feel like part of the community. The only reason why they made me President was because you wouldn't take it. I just get up there and do the best I can."

"Stop being so modest," Apolonio chided him. "You're a born leader. Just imagine what things would have been like if you hadn't come here with Isidro and Emmanuel. The three of you would still have been on the Islands, and none of this would have happened. Look at those four boys of yours. They have wonderful lives ahead of them. Whenever they have doubts about themselves, they'll look back at your life as an inspiration. Every one of them has your spirit, the will to succeed. You've got that fire, Dulfo, and you've given it to those boys. Mark my words, the whole world will be touched by those boys someday, and you'll look back with pride."

"You could sell sun tan lotion to a Moro," Teodulfo chuckled, shaking his head. "I do appreciate your vote of confidence, believe me. Sometimes I get down on myself, a poor house boy trying to make ends meet. Sometimes I wonder what it's all about, how I came all this way just to cook and clean like a lowly servant."

"That's what it's all about, serving others and helping others," Apolonio insisted. "Look what happened to Emmanuel, rest his soul. Always trying to prove himself, always thinking that might makes right. Look at your brothers-in-law, they're in and out of prison these days. See what happened to Isidro, trying to cut corners and beat the system. The honest man, the man who endures, is the man who stores up the real treasures in life. Those kids of yours will always look back and remember what you did. This community will look back at what you did. Don't you ever sell yourself short. You made all these things possible. You are my most trusted friend, Teodulfo, and there will never be another."

Teodulfo was entirely unprepared for the next event that would shake his world that holiday season. Colonel Sibley announced that he planned to retire and move to Arizona. He had already recommended Teodulfo to one of his close friends, Joe Couch, who was expecting him to start work that Monday. Couch lived off South New Braunfels Avenue, a distance from Fort Sam but equidistant from Can't Stop in the opposite direction.

"I—I don't know what to say," Teodulfo was dumbfounded. "This is so sudden. I had no idea I was going to have to go to work for someone else that I don't even know."

"Don't you worry yourself about it," Sibley remained jovial. "Joe Couch is one of my oldest friends. I knew Joe before I was deployed to the Philippines. He's a swell guy, you'll get along with him just fine."

"Well, gee, I was kinda thinking that when I got done working for you, I might try to make my way up in the world. I can't be a house boy all my life."

"Now, see here, Dulfo, you don't want to get too full of yourself," Sibley advised him. "You know we're living in some tough times here. Lots of families are living hand-to-mouth trying to make ends meet. You've got a wife and kids, that's a lot of responsibility. You're starting to think that being a house boy isn't a worthwhile position. Well, don't forget you've been working at the home of a Colonel in the United States Army, that's nothing to sniff at. It's a damn sight better than washing dishes or scrubbing toilets like most other Filipinos. I've always watched out for your interests. Wasn't I brought you over here in the first place?"

"That's true, sir, and I'll never forget that."

"We've always treated you like part of the family. We let you go home early and even gave you time off when you needed it. We even gave you turkeys for the family on Thanksgiving and Christmas. How many times did we let you take the leftovers after parties? And, of course, you have to consider the fact that you've been more of a tidier than a housecleaner. Mrs. Sibley is a very clean woman, you must admit, and left you with as little to clean up after as possible."

"I would most certainly agree, sir."

"Let me assure you that Mrs. Couch is just as fine a woman as you'll ever meet, and that Joe will be just as generous and fair towards you as I've been. Why, who knows, once your boys get old enough to go to work, I wouldn't be surprised if Joe would be able to help them find jobs as house boys themselves. Don't you worry, Dulfo. Things will work out just fine."

And so Teodulfo left the employ of the Sibleys, reporting to the Couch home that next week, counting his blessings and wondering if he was coming up short.

It was the next week when he learned there was a new member of the household. He came home from work that Friday and found out the boys had adopted a kitten. It was one of those orange-and-whites that roamed the neighborhood, and for some odd reason they named him Kincaid. Apparently Kincaid was getting the run of the house, and Teodulfo was in no mood when he got home that afternoon.

"Doesn't anyone ask my permission about these kind of things anymore?" he griped at Stella when she came into their bedroom after he changed to his house slippers. "What the heck were you thinking of, letting them bring a cat in here?"

"They love the poor thing," she insisted. "What's the harm of them having something in here to put a smile on their faces? Why should it be that they can only come home to your sour puss every day?"

"Yeah, if you had to do what I do, you wouldn't have such an attitude."

"Is that right? I wash clothes for six people in a basin, cook for six people in a tiny kitchen, clean the outhouse..."

"You can start adding to your list of complaints, only you'll have no one to blame but yourself. Those things shed hair, so you'll be sweeping cat hair from everything. Their piss is like acid, you can smell it in the next room. Plus they eat, so now you have to buy cat food. And they eat meat, they don't eat rice and beans."

"That's good. At least one of us will be eating better."

"What did you just say?" he demanded as she pranced out of the room.

He sat there, trying to control his temper as he wiped sweat from his brow. He was in his late twenties and felt as if life was passing him by. The words of Colonel Sibley gnawed at his stomach after their conversation of several days ago. Was this all there was? Joe Couch was a good enough fellow, and Mrs. Couch was very civil. Only it grated at his nerves every time a visitor came by and introduced their 'new house boy'. What happened next, would he be promoted to 'yard man' someday? Maybe 'cook' had a little more prestige to it.

Stella finally began calling everyone in for dinner, and the table was quiet as he liked it when he sat down for supper. The boys learned a long time ago that the table was for eating, not for chattering. Stella served the food and finally sat down at the opposite end of the table, while the boys sat on either side. Manuel sat next to baby Freddie to help him mind his manners, and Dolfo and Daniel tolerated each other when their elbows did not bump together.

The meal was eaten in near-silence as was the custom, and they all asked for permission to be excused once their plates were wiped clean. Stella gathered the dishes and began the chore of washing them along with the cooking pots and pans. Teodulfo sat there for a while, thinking of how he would sneak up behind her and fondle her, dragging her into the bedroom with him. When did they stop doing that? He couldn't even remember.

Time at the Couches dragged on as if being behind prison walls, while the hours after work blew by like the wind. He switched on the radio serials, and Dolfo was spellbound by the new Buck Rogers serial. They listened as Buck and Wilma Deering battled Killer Kane and the forces of evil. Teodulfo wished a space ship would pick up his family from the Islands and bring them over here. Dolfo fantasized about being the one who flew over and got them.

Finally the boys came in for the night and Stella made sure they all took a bath before scrubbing down baby Freddie and putting him to bed. Teodulfo gave strict orders that Kincaid was to be put out for the night. He would always go out and make sure the kitten had water and kitchen scraps before he went to bed. Only on this particular night, Kincaid was nowhere to be found. He stormed into the house, switching on the lights in the living room and the porch where the boys' cots were set up.

"All right, where's that darn cat!" he demanded. Stella came out of the bedroom, filled with trepidation in knowing someone was in deep trouble. She watched as he went from cot to cot, yanking off their sheets. He went to Dolfo first, then Manuel, where he found the kitten cradled in his arms. Dolfo took the kitten from him and put it outside, then came back and pulled Manuel to his feet.

"What the heck is wrong with you? How dare you disobey me?"

Manuel refused to respond, and Teodulfo gave him a swat on the butt. He remained silent, and Teodulfo slapped him in the head. The boy's face seemed ready to explode into tears, but still he would not give in. Teodulfo shoved past Stella and retrieved his belt as the other boys hid their faces in their pillows.

"Now, are you going to tell me why you brought that cat in here?"

The eleven-year-old was the toughest of his sons, and he would be damned if he backed down in this test of wills. He began laying the strap onto his son's buttocks, and could not believe the boy would not explain his actions. Stella's heart was torn as she watched her favorite son endure the beating, which appeared as if it was not going to end.

Finally the boy exploded with a feral scream, as if possessed by the spirit of the Moro, the spirit of his godfather Hercules. He raised his face to the ceiling and cried out in pain, in rage, resentment, anguish. Teodulfo stepped back, his jaws slack with astonishment at the sight. Stella could take no more and drowned the boy's screams against her bosom. Teodulfo numbly laid the strap down on the coffee table and made his way out the back door.

Darned Moro. Where on earth did he get that from?

Teodulfo found the kitten lying on the steps and picked it up, holding it in his arms as he sat down on the chair beneath the canopy. He felt as if he was losing control of his life, and didn't know how to get it back. Manuel was going to be a teenager in a couple of years, then Daniel right behind him. They had already chosen a sport in which they beat other men down with their gloved fists. How was he going to control them then? How would he feed them? What would happen when Dolfo went on to high school, then college, and brought his fiancée home and introduced her to his father, the house boy?

"I put the boys back to bed, Dulfo. Come inside, you have work tomorrow."

He heard Stella's voice through the screen door but did not turn to face her. He continued to stroke the kitten's back staring up at the silvery moon.

"You go to bed," he said quietly. "I'll be along."

Stella went back inside and finally dozed off. She fell into a deep sleep, trying to put her husband's spiritual turmoil out of her mind. She knew the inner frustration and helplessness of a man whose life was slipping through his fingers. Her father died in Mexico from a similar sense of despair, after arriving from Spain and finding that he had come to even less than he had left. Juan Munoz died a broken man, and Jacoba Munoz would never leave the land where he died. She would never see that her children were flourishing in America, and the hope that lived inside her grandchildren.

She got out of bed and saw the sunrise. She found herself alone and realized Teodulfo never came back inside. She had an urge to tell him they needed to bring the boys to Mexico to meet their grandmother. He needed to realize the future awaiting their children. He could not limit his vision to what laid before him. He needed to see past that, to the horizon that they would reach in their lifetimes. That was what it was all about.

She could have never know there was a tiny time bomb inside his head, planted there by nature back before he was born. It was an aneurysm, a wall in an artery in his brain that exploded, killing him on the spot. He appeared as if sleeping, the kitten still lying peacefully in his lap. She put her fingers beneath his nose, felt beneath his ear, felt his chest. It was finished. His days as a house boy were over.

She stared out at the sunrise and promised herself that the sons of Teodulfo David Dizon would make their mark in San

Antonio and beyond. She would remind them of the story of the brash young man who met her in a club one night, eloped with her, made himself a pillar of his communities and founded the Filipino-American Society. She would live long enough to tell her grandchildren, and maybe even their children.

She would make sure that Teodulfo David Dizon would never be forgotten.

Dear reader,

We hope you enjoyed reading *Bical*. Please take a moment to leave a review in Amazon, even if it's a short one. Your opinion is important to us.

Discover more books by John Reinhard Dizon at https://www.nextchapter.pub/authors/john-reinhard-dizon

Want to know when one of our books is free or discounted for Kindle? Join the newsletter at http://eepurl.com/bqqB3H

Best regards,
John Reinhard Dizon and the Next Chapter Team

You might also like:

Starting Over by Ronald Bagliere

To read the first chapter for free, head to:
https://www.nextchapter.pub/books/starting-over-
contemporary-fiction

CPSIA information can be obtained
at www.ICGtesting.com
Printed in the USA
BVHW041527180121
598054BV00016B/489/J

9 781034 257615